ECHOES OF THE
WHITE GIRAFFE

D1009364

OTHER YEARLING BOOKS YOU WILL ENJOY:

YEARLING BOOKS/YOUNG YEARLINGS/YEARLING CLASSICS are designed especially to entertain and enlighten young people. Patricia Reilly Giff, consultant to this series, received her bachelor's degree from Marymount College and a master's degree in history from St. John's University. She holds a Professional Diploma in Reading and a Doctorate of Humane Letters from Hofstra University. She was a teacher and reading consultant for many years, and is the author of numerous books for young readers.

For a complete listing of all Yearling titles, write to
Dell Readers Service,
P.O. Box 1045,
South Holland, IL 60473.

ECHOES OF THE WHITE GIRAFFE

SOOK NYUL CHOI

A Yearling Book

In memory of Nungho and his dreams
and
To Audrey and Kathy with love

In tribute to the brave veterans of the Korean
War, to those who gave their lives in battle, and
to all the unsung heroes and heroines who
endured those sad and difficult years.

Published by
Bantam Doubleday Dell Books for Young Readers
a division of
Bantam Doubleday Dell Publishing Group, Inc.
1540 Broadway
New York, New York 10036

If you purchased this book without a cover you should be aware that this book is
stolen property. It was reported as "unsold and destroyed" to the publisher and nei-
ther the author nor the publisher has received any payment for this "stripped book."

Copyright © 1993 by Sook Nyul Choi

All rights reserved. No part of this book may be reproduced or transmitted in any
form or by any means, electronic or mechanical, including photocopying, recording,
or by any information storage and retrieval system, without the written permission
of the Publisher, except where permitted by law. For information address Houghton
Mifflin Company, New York, New York 10003.

The trademark Yearling® is registered in the U.S. Patent and Trademark Office.

The trademark Dell® is registered in the U.S. Patent and Trademark Office.

ISBN: 0-440-40970-5

Reprinted by arrangement with Houghton Mifflin Company
Printed in the United States of America

March 1995

10 9 8 7 6 5 4 3 2 1

Acknowledgments

I am deeply touched by the warm reception my first book *Year of Impossible Goodbyes* received. I would like to thank the many librarians across the country for their enthusiasm; their letters, phone calls, and invitations to visit and read at their libraries provided me encouragement during the lonely days writing this book. The enthusiasm of my old and new friends at the Women's National Book Association over my first book, and their frequent inquiries as to my progress on this sequel has been a source of strength. And again, my sincere thanks to my editor and friend, Laura Hornik, for her continued interest in my work.

My heartfelt thanks to my daughters, Audrey and Kathy, for their frank critiques and for their constant loving support.

Sook Nyul Choi
Cambridge, 1993

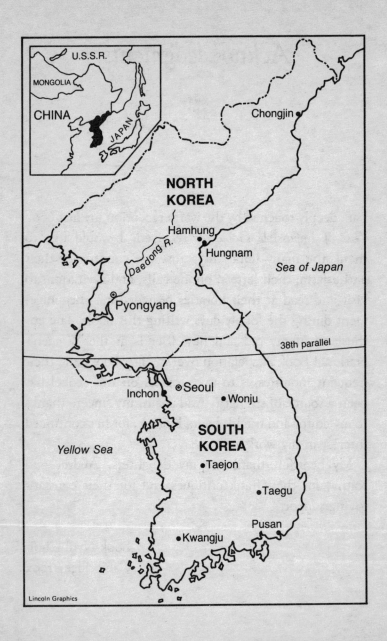

Chapter One

The sun was setting and a faint breeze stirred over our flushed faces as we put down the last of the sand bags. Two wood-frame single classroom buildings finally stood before us. Father Lee, my younger brother Inchun, and all the teachers and students stood staring in silence as they proudly beheld the grand buildings. As Teacher Yun gazed at the first classroom, see seemed to caress every beam, board, and brick with her large dark eyes. She then turned to the second classroom, and again, lovingly examined every inch of it, from top to bottom. I could almost tell which pieces of brick, wood, and concrete my best friend Bokhi and I had carried. "Oh, I can't stand it anymore," one girl finally shouted with excitement. "I want to go inside and walk around."

The teachers smiled as they watched us rush into the classrooms. How proud we were to have helped build our very own school. My shoulders and back ached, and my callused hands throbbed. Hot tears flooded my eyes. I was exhausted, but it was a happy exhaustion, and I felt overjoyed.

"You all go home early for a change," said Teacher Yun. "Let us teachers take care of the rest. No need for you to come back this weekend. We will finish up, and on Monday, we can use our new classrooms."

Our teachers were so thoughtful to let us all go home and have the weekend to ourselves. This would be the first Saturday and Sunday we would not be working at the site since construction had begun several months before.

How glad we had been when Teacher Yun first found this small plot by the seashore, in an area of Pusan where many refugees, including Bokhi, had settled. Teacher Yun and a few other teachers from the Ewha School in Seoul had managed to flee to Pusan, and they were anxious to teach refugee students like Bokhi and me. We were even more anxious to resume our studies. We had not attended any school since the war began, over eight months earlier. Pusan was so crowded that there was no place for us to gather and study, so we had decided to build our own classrooms. When Teacher Yun found this site, we quickly began to build our small school, using whatever materials we could find. We collected driftwood, bricks, stones, rocks, pebbles, and even shells. We carried these things to the building site, while we dreamed of having a place to sit and study, protected from the monsoon rains, the howling winds, and the scorchingly hot sun. Now that dream stood right before us.

Wonderful as it was to see the two rooms finished,

suddenly, I couldn't help feeling a strange sadness deep within me. Our country was still at war, and we were still refugees here in Pusan. I felt sad at how content we were with these two simple wood-frame buildings. I wondered what had become of our beautiful brick Ewha School in Seoul, with its sparkling classrooms and its beautifully tiered garden. Maybe we could make a small garden in front of these humbler classrooms, I thought.

Inchun put away his tools and nails and we headed toward the refugee information center where Mother worked. As we dragged our tired feet through the streets of Pusan, we passed many Pusan School students. Swinging their book bags and chatting like magpies, they looked so energetic and carefree. Their school uniforms were clean and freshly pressed. I looked at Inchun's work clothes and my own. No one would think that we, too, were students. I thought of the happy days before the war when I used to run out my front door each morning dressed in my school uniform: a navy blue skirt and a white blouse, proudly adorned with a silver school pin embossed with a pear blossom, the *ewha*. The war had even robbed me of my school pin.

I sighed sadly. Inchun looked at me and shrugged his shoulders with resignation. So, we are refugees, he seemed to say. The war broke out in Seoul and we couldn't help it. We had no choice but to flee south to Pusan, away from the bombing and fighting.

When we approached the small gray house that housed Father Lee's church and the refugee information center,

Mother came rushing out. "Stay there, I'm coming! We must hurry so we can climb the mountain before the sun goes down." Knitting her brow, she looked up at the setting sun. "We need to fetch some water from the well tonight, too. I went at dawn, but the water line was already too long."

By the way Mother rattled on, I knew she had not received news about Father or my brothers. We hadn't heard a thing since our separation from them. Were they still alive? Were they trying to contact us? Each day, many new notices went up on the already crowded information board at the refugee information center. Whenever I passed by, I stopped to read the notes myself. "Looking for my brother Chang Kyu. I am at our cousin's house. Your third sister," said one. Another said, "Dear Sung, your wife has been injured, but is still alive and is recovering. Contact Father Lee. Your Uncle Ho."

Every day, Mother feverishly wrote down any information she heard and contacted people for any possible additional clues. Each time she successfully reunited one family, she was filled with renewed hope that our family would soon be reunited, too, and she enthusiastically told us all about it. But today she pursed her lips and walked quickly toward the refugee mountain where we lived. Her face was drawn and expressionless, as if she were too upset to show the slightest emotion.

In an attempt to cheer her up, I said, "Mother, our classroom buildings are finally standing."

Mother smiled and patted me on the head. "You all

worked so hard. It's about time to hit the books now."

We fell silent again as we wove through the clean streets of Pusan toward the steep, jagged mountain at the edge of the city. I was tired, and I felt a tightness in my legs from the long day's work. Looking at the low brick houses we passed so quickly, I wished one of them were ours. The smell of rice, hot beef broth, and sweet peppers wafted out one of the windows. A woman called to her children, and suddenly a little boy and girl shot past me. They pushed open the low wooden gate and rushed in. I thought of our beautiful house in Seoul.

A blue marble rolled toward me, and as I stooped to pick it up, the little girl came running back. I handed it to her, and thought how lucky she was. I must have been staring at her, for she looked at me uncomfortably and dashed back in, calling to her mother. Yellowed lace curtains hung in the windows, and red geraniums bloomed in the wooden flower box, faded and covered with a layer of rich green moss. Everything bore signs of the tranquil passage of time. What a soothing and reassuring sight for me after seeing my whole world destroyed by bombs and enemy tanks. The sounds and smells of peace surrounded me. I took a deep breath and realized how grateful I should be to walk without fear on such a peaceful old street. Though my feet ached and my shoulders were stiff, I decided never to complain about life as a refugee in Pusan.

After walking through many side streets, we finally reached the foot of the mountain. Mother quietly got ready for the climb, pulling up her long skirt, called a *chima*, and tightening the string around her waist.

"I don't want to get red mud on my slacks," Inchun said as he rolled up his pants legs.

I stared at the steep mountain before me. How ominously it loomed above us. Rows and rows of small plywood shacks covered the barren red-brown mountain from the bottom to the very top. As we were among the last to arrive in Pusan, our place was at the very top and we had the longest way to climb.

"*Nuna*, let's go. You always stare up at the mountain as if you were seeing it for the first time," Inchun said to me impatiently.

I shot him a disapproving look for speaking to me, his *nuna* (meaning "older sister"), that way. "I can't help it," I said measuredly. "The height and steepness still amaze me." The mountain always seemed to be standing straight up, defying me to climb it.

"Come on Sookan, we are not going to get there unless you start moving your feet," Mother said as she gently reminded me of the old saying, "The eyes say, 'oh, no,' but the feet say 'one step at a time and you'll be there in no time.' "

It began to drizzle. Inchun squinted up at the dark sky and said with a wry smile, "Well, pretty soon, our hands will start talking, too — saying 'One grab at a time, we will get there sometime.' "

On rainy days, we had to get down on all fours to

climb up the muddy, treeless mountainside. Inchun, with his long legs, bounded up the mountain with a look of determination, and Mother followed. I reluctantly began the long trip up with a sigh. Although I promised myself not to complain, it was hard to be cheerful about climbing in the rain. I was already so tired that I could barely manage putting one foot in front of the other. As Inchun and Mother walked ahead of me, small pebbles came loose, rolled down the mountainside, and pelted me in the ankles. My worn sneakers were no help on this slippery terrain. I kept losing my footing and tried to dig my nails into the earth to keep from falling. My palms and fingertips throbbed, and the red mud caked on my shoes made me feel very heavy. There was no sense in scraping the mud off; it would only accumulate again after another few steps.

Suddenly Mother slid past me with her arms outstretched as she looked for something to grab hold of. Completely losing her balance, she fell, rolled down the hill sideways, bumped into the wall of a little shack at the next crevice in the mountain, and then landed with a thump on her behind. Her hairpin had been dislodged, and her long braid hung down to her waist. Her *chima* was caked with red mountain mud. Her handsome oval face was ashen, and she sat stupefied, looking down at herself. Then, embarrassed, she desperately began fixing her hair, straightening her *chima*, and scraping the mud from her sleeves.

All I could do was stand there and look at her; it had all happened so fast. She was so frail that I was terrified she had hurt herself. Mother had fallen many times in our last few months here on the mountain, but never all the way down like this. Inchun ran after her, sliding and tripping, and almost landed on top of her. Stunned, they stared at each other, then looked up at me.

"Are you hurt Mother?" I yelled down to her.

"We're all right," she shouted back.

Pensively, she sat there pulling the clumps of mud from her *chima*. She looked around her and smiled with resignation. Then suddenly, she tossed her arms way up, tilted her head back, and started to laugh hysterically. She laughed until tears came running down her cheeks. Deep laugh lines emanated from the corners of her closed eyes and covered her cheeks as unbridled laughter spilled forth from her wide-open mouth. It was the first time I had heard my mother laugh so heartily.

My heart pounded with a strange mixture of relief and anger. Then I heard my own laughter burst forth, too. I laughed uncontrollably, wiping the tears from my eyes. What else was there to do? What was the sense of getting angry? The war had brought us here to be taunted by this giant mountain. We were helpless. All we could do was laugh, pick ourselves up, and start all over again.

I saw Inchun watch us with a bewildered smile. He stood calmly, waiting for us to get up and continue the climb up the mountain. Although he was only twelve, three years younger than I, he acted as though he were the oldest, the leader and protector of our small family. He was painfully aware of the fact that he was the only male, now that we had not heard from Father and our three older brothers since we fled Seoul.

The drizzling stopped. Peeking through the slow-moving gray clouds, the setting sun spread its last glorious rays of orange and red upon the rows of little plywood houses. We continued climbing hurriedly and passed the only well on this side of the mountain. A long line of women and children stood there, holding buckets, bottles, and jars. Many women had small babies tied to their backs, and we could see the silhouettes of these young mothers swaying back and forth as they tried to soothe the crying babies.

I watched the shadows of these tired-looked figures and felt sad, for I knew Inchun and I would soon be a part of that line. Mother drew most of the water we needed at dawn when the line was shortest, but Inchun and I often fetched the water for the evening cooking. Even though we carried bucketfuls each day, we never had enough water to skip a day.

In silence, we kept climbing. We passed a woman bent over a small wire-frame stove. A baby was tied on her back with a large cotton strap, and as the mother leaned over to blow on the little pile of twigs to get the fire going, the smoke wafted into the baby's face, making it

9

yelp with discomfort. At the next shack, an old man was fiercely sweeping the little patch of red dirt that was his front yard.

From the front door of our hut, we could see all the way down the mountain. Our home consisted of one room made of four thin plywood walls with a sliding door separating a small kitchen area from the main part of the room. Behind the shack, there was a steep drop-off, and it seemed as if a strong wind could blow our house off the mountain into the jagged crags below. Across the way was another mountain, also studded with rows and rows of refugee huts. The sun had already gone down, and as I looked down the mountain, I saw dark shadows moving about. Feeling afraid that the dark valley might swallow me, I quickly sat on the little wooden ledge by the sliding rice-paper paneled door, and looked down at the city of Pusan.

The pale round moon rose over the mountain, and the stars were sprinkled about the sky. Here at the top of the mountain, I felt very close to the moon and stars as I gazed down at the hundreds of dwellings now softly blanketed by darkness. Flickering candlelight danced out from some of the little houses and cast a warm glow on the plain plywood walls. The clinking and clanking of dinner being prepared and the low murmur of dinner conversation filled the air like a comforting tune. The moon rose higher and more stars appeared overhead.

I pretended that the ugly huts were special guest houses for the stars that came to visit Earth for the night. "Inchun, bring the bottles and bucket out," I called, suddenly feeling warm and happy. "The moon is bright enough for us to see our way. Let's go and fetch some water."

Inchun and I, swinging the empty buckets, headed down to the water line. "Sit down and rest while waiting your turn," Mother called while chasing after us. She handed us two small apples to munch on while we waited.

Chapter Two

The early morning light began creeping through the cracks in the rice-paper paneled door. Stretching out over the wooden rafters, the slivers of light danced overhead. From under the door, a wider beam of light glistening with color shone through, intersecting the dancing rays. The fusion of these beams of vibrant light turned the walls into a wondrous canvas. But the cold wind seeping through those same crevices made me close my eyes again, and draw my knees into my chest to curl up under the thin blanket. I wanted to sleep a bit longer before heading down to fetch water.

Suddenly, a voice rang out through the sleepy mountain.

"Good morning, all you refugees. Good morning! Rise up and greet the sun!"

The mountain echoed, "morning . . . morning . . . rise, rise . . . greet the sun, sun, sun . . ."

I sat up, my eyes wide with delight. I turned toward the far right side of the room where Inchun lay. With his head resting on his folded arms, he was staring up at the beams of light dancing on the ceiling.

"Inchun, what was that? Who said that?" I asked excitedly.

"Yeah, yeah, yeah, I heard. Why get so excited? It's probably a crazy man, probably a crazy poet who thinks nothing of waking people up at dawn," Inchun said flatly. But I saw how his dark eyes twinkled. He, too, was hoping to hear more. I even saw his toes wiggle with restless anticipation.

To our delight, the voice bellowed forth again, this time louder and stronger.

"Hello, all you refugees on these mountains. Rise and shine. Remember it is a new day, a brand new day. Hello, hello."

The happy mountain called back, "shine . . . and shine. A new day, new day . . . hello, hello, hello."

How deep and resonant his voice was! How sweetly it reverberated through the mountain, slowly dissipating in the vast morning sky.

The sleepy mountain came alive. I heard some men grumble and cough loudly. An old man who lived below us grumbled, "So early in the morning! Be quiet, you, you rice bucket!"

"Old man, you're waking up my grandchild. You hush!" an old woman from another hut farther down the mountain yelled out. Babies were crying, and pots and pans were clanking as the young women set about making breakfast. The thin plywood walls and rice-paper doors didn't muffle any noise. I felt as if I were in the middle of one big room with everyone else.

I was itching with curiosity. I wanted to see this bold and enchanting man. How rude of all these refugees not to respond to his friendly greeting. Only the mountain had responded to him. I wanted to shout back a morning greeting myself. What did he look like? Which mountain top was he shouting from? I imagined a strong and handsome, but tormented, poet with so much more than a morning greeting pent up inside him. I could picture him standing bravely at the top of a mountain with white fluffy clouds overhead, and his echoes wafting around him. How grand it would be to see him and to shout back at him. I should. I must.

I jumped out of bed and dashed outside, ignoring In-chun's wide-eyed stare. I went around to the back of our shack and climbed the remainder of the way to the very top of our mountain. For the first time, I was happy that our little house was the very last one on this side of the mountain. It took over an hour to climb up here from the streets of Pusan city, but now, with a little hop, I was at the very top, where the view was clear.

Standing on the other mountain top was a thin man in a white T-shirt with his head cocked way back to face the blue skies and with his hands cupped over his mouth. He shouted another morning greeting, and then cupped his hands around his right ear to hear his greeting echo through the mountains.

Standing on tiptoe, I stretched my arms way over my head and waved them back and forth. Jumping up and down, I shouted as loud as I could, "H–e–l–l–o, h–e–l–l–o, good morning to you, too!"

"Oh, hello, little girl. You have a great day!" He shouted back with delight, waving his arms wildly. His enthusiastic response made me jump with excitement. I cupped my hands around my mouth just as he had. I wanted to shout to him, "Are you a mountain poet?"

Mother suddenly grabbed me, and whispered harshly, "What on earth are you doing? A grown-up girl shouting at the top of her lungs, and so early in the morning, too. What a crazy thing to do! What a disgrace! One more step backward and you might even have fallen."

I was so enchanted by the shouting poet, I hadn't seen Mother storm up the mountain. Her face was flushed and she was panting. She held my hand firmly, dragged me home, and pulled me inside, shutting the door tightly behind her.

Inchun took one look at my ghostly white face and erupted with laughter. Pointing his long, bony finger at me, he laughed so hard he doubled over. Nearly choking with laughter, he gasped, "Mother, you have to watch out for *Nuna*. She is just as mad as that crazy shouting poet. *Nuna*'s poetic heart knows no shame and has no sense." He pounded on his knee with one hand, and held his stomach with the other, as tears of laughter pooled in his eyes. "I am not going down the mountain with you this morning, *Nuna*. Oh, how embarrassing, how embarrassing! How I wish I had a camera. What a sight it was, what a sight!"

Mother's stern face softened and laugh lines appeared around her dark almond eyes. She covered her mouth to stifle her laughter, and then, looking in my direction, she forced a stern look back on her face. "Sookan, my dear, sit down next to me. Listen very carefully. It is a disgrace for a well-brought-up girl to shout like that with such abandon. You are a young lady now. You cannot afford to be so impulsive anymore. People are going to say you are growing up wild and without manners because you have no father and no older brothers. I expect you to behave like a proper young lady at all times. Do you understand?"

Mother felt the absence of my father and three older brothers in every facet of our lives. I, too, thought of them often and missed their presence, especially when I saw children in Pusan walking by with their fathers and older siblings. That always looked like such a perfect picture. My family wasn't perfect anymore. I often felt lonesome, sad, and scared.

The hut we lived in always felt empty somehow, and I liked hearing the sound of a man's voice, even if it were that of a crazy shouting poet, a total stranger. His hearty morning greeting made me feel safe and happy somehow. Despite Mother's reprimand, I hoped that someday I would meet that brave and unusual man. There were many questions I wanted to ask him.

Inchun was still grinning, shaking his head in disbelief as he stared at me. Mother looked pale and drained as she quietly looked down at her clasped hands. I felt silly in front of Inchun, and I was ashamed that I had worried Mother. "Shall I go down to fetch some water before I go?" I asked, hoping to distract her.

"Oh, no! You two are due at church soon. I'll take care of the water. I am getting quite good at balancing the jug on my head these days," she said with a forced smile.

I tied a bag containing my good shoes securely around my waist, and started down the mountain. Tilting my body backwards, I held my arms out for balance and took each step cautiously to avoid sliding. Halfway down the mountain, I passed the long line of women waiting for water from the well. All those women standing patiently in line suddenly seemed to me like bold heroines waging a daily battle, determined to win just one day at a time. I knew how difficult it was. Carrying the water uphill was the worst part. The bucket was always half empty by the time I got up to our small hut.

A thin woman with a jug of water poised on her head and a baby tied to her back walked past me. The baby hung heavily on her back, and the cotton strap knotted tightly in front made her look so fragile. She breathed rapidly, and her face was red. With her eyes glued to the ground and her arms outstretched, she carefully moved forward. I watched her in admiration as she passed me and went up the hill. When she reached the slippery part, she held the water jug in place with her right hand and put her other hand on the baby's back to soothe him.

Noticing the sun way up in the mountain sky, I started running down the mountain. I would rather risk falling and bruising myself than walk in late and have Haerin, the choir conductor, roll her eyes at me. After a good deal of skidding, I finally reached the bottom of the mountain, where I stopped to make myself presentable. I wiped the dirt from my face, smoothed my hair, and beat my blouse and skirt to get rid of the fine mist of red dust that had settled on me. Then, I hurriedly took off my grimy sneakers.

Just then, I heard someone whistling a familiar tune. I turned and saw Inchun, looking cool and collected. His dark hair was neatly combed in place, his white shirt was crisp and fresh, and his city shoes shone. He looked as if he had just stepped out of one of the houses on the city street.

"I saw you dawdling and watching the women at the water line," he teased. "You didn't even see me speed past you, did you?"

I glared at him, annoyed at his composure while I was still busily emptying the pebbles from my sneakers. Despite what he had said earlier about not wanting to be seen with me, he had been waiting for me.

While I put my city walking shoes on, he said, "Hurry

up! Father Lee is waiting for me. I have to help him break in a new altar boy, since I am getting too tall and too busy with my science classes these days." I gave him another sour look for bragging about his height. I looked so short walking next to him.

Under the warm morning sun, we walked toward the church in silence. I swung my shoebag, and was happy as I rushed to keep up with my younger brother's long strides. When Inchun, Father Lee, and the other boys from Inchun's school were helping us to build Ewha, Inchun and I always walked home together. But now we did not get to be with each other often, since he went to the all-boys' school and I went to Ewha, the all-girls' school, and after classes, we were both busy with our school projects. Now Inchun spent most of his afternoons and even weekends with his favorite teacher, the one who taught science.

I often wished that he would join the choir, for that was the one thing that we might be able to do together. But I think Inchun was tone deaf. It was a strange phenomenon that I did not understand. He whistled beautifully; the melody and rhythm were perfect, and he whistled with such feeling, eliciting just the right emotion. But when he sang, he was somehow always miserably out of tune. I once laughed at him, thinking he did it on purpose. But after I laughed, I never heard him sing again.

I wondered if I should ask him to sing a song for me

now, just to see if anything had changed. But I decided to keep him company in silence. I knew Inchun better: he probably tested himself often in private to see if he could sing. If there were any change, he would surprise me with a beautiful song in perfect tune, and would smile deeply as I looked at him with awe.

Chapter Three

The choir members stood at attention in the back of our one-room church. When Haerin, the conductor, waved her baton, our choir practice began. As I followed the exaggerated movements of her baton, the words of the Shouting Poet kept ringing in my ears. "Good morning, refugees . . . refugees . . . refugees." It resonated so sweetly through the mountains. The word "refugee" rang as melodiously as all the other words, not sounding as cold and ugly as it had the first time I heard it, the first time I met Haerin. My mind raced back to that unforgettable day, our first day in Pusan.

We had escaped the bombing in Seoul just three days before and had spent an entire day walking in the bitter cold all the way to Inchon harbor. From there, a small rowboat carried us out to a large ship. In the ship's bowels, we rode for hours until we reached Pusan. Famished, frostbitten, and dirty, we made our way to the base of the refugee mountain. In our tattered, filthy clothes, we stared up at the steep, jagged, red-brown mountain looming above us. Exhausted and overwhelmed, we did not know what to do.

I looked over at a brick house at the foot of the mountain. Shaded by leafy persimmon and apricot trees, and enclosed by a low brick wall covered with morning glories, it looked safe and comfortable. The shiny brass door knockers on the big wooden door shimmered in the sunlight, reminding me of our dark cherry-wood doors at home in Seoul with the two brass door knockers shaped like dragons. This house was not as big and grand as our house in Seoul had been, but it looked so inviting that I wished someone would ask us in to rest.

I could hear the clanking of dishes and the murmur of voices. How wonderfully peaceful life seemed here. Yet visions of bombs, burning trees, and smoldering buildings kept filling my head, and the horrible smell of smoke and death stayed with me. I shook my head from side to side, trying to rid myself of these horrible memories. Feeling miserable and helpless, I started to cry.

"Shhhhh, everything will be fine," Mother said as she hugged me. "Don't think of the past. We have to move forward and figure out what to do. Now, let's just start climbing. We have a place to stay at the very top." Placing me in front of her, she held me tight, and together, we gazed up at the ominous mountain.

A brown dog ran out into the yard of the house I had been gazing at so wistfully. Speeding toward us, it jumped up to rest its paws on the low wall and barked furiously. Its deep brown eyes and short brown coat reminded me of my boxer Luxy in Seoul. I went over and patted him and he immediately lowered his head, whimpered, and wagged his long thin tail. I thought of my boxer's stubby tail that wagged so busily, forming little pools of wrinkles on her back.

The door of the house opened, and a girl in a bright pink lace dress ran out. She grimaced when she saw us, and said, "Browny, come here! Stop barking at the refugees. They all have to come this way now. They can't find another path up the mountain. Come over here!" She shot a disdainful glance my way, and as the dog rushed in, she shut the door and quickly disappeared. But her shrill voice rang in my head. She had called me a "refugee." That's what I am now, I thought to myself. How terrible the word *refugee* sounded! She said it as if it were the name of some horrible disease. A chill ran down my spine, and I shivered. Through tear-filled eyes, I stared down at my torn shoes and dirty clothes. I fingered my stiff, dusty hair, which had not been washed since we left Seoul. My body ached, and my head pounded as my new name echoed through my mind. "Refugee, refugee, refugee."

I hoped that I would never lay eyes on the girl again, and I vowed to stay clear of her house every time I climbed the mountain. But it wasn't meant to be. A month later, Father Lee asked me to join a choir he was forming with members from Pusan High School for Boys, Pusan Girls' School, and students from Seoul. He thought it would be a good idea for us to get to know each other better; we might be in Pusan for longer than we had hoped. There was someone special he wanted me to meet, he said; someone with whom he thought I would have a great deal in common. We were about the same age, he noted. Haerin was sixteen, only one year my senior. We were both fond of music and loved to sing. So, at the refugee information center, Father Lee introduced me to a tall girl with long silky hair and unusually long bangs that gave some balance to her thin face and framed her protruding eyes. She stood proudly in her Pusan Girls' School uniform, with hymnals under one arm and a thin black leather case under the other. I immediately recognized her as Browny's owner.

I lowered my eyes and fumbled for something in my pocket. I didn't know what to do or say. My face burned, and I knew that even my neck had turned an embarrassing pink.

"Sookan," Father Lee said, "I've been wanting you to meet Haerin. She will be the conductor of our choir. You two will have a lot to talk about. You can teach each other about your homes. Haerin knows all about Pusan. She has lived here her whole life."

When I mustered enough courage to look her in the eyes, I realized that she had no recollection of having ever met me. She stared at me with blank disinterest.

From then on, I had seen Haerin several hours every Saturday for choir practice, and four hours every Sunday, when we sang at four Masses. There were twenty-five choir members, seventeen boys and only eight girls. I knew a few of the girls by sight, but I didn't know any of the boys. It wasn't proper for girls and boys to talk, unless, of course, there was a legitimate reason to do so. All the boys stood to the left of the organ, and all the girls stood to the right, just as all the men sat on the left side of the church at Mass and all the women sat on the right. Most of the boys in the choir were from Pusan and I had never seen them before.

However, I had noticed one handsome boy who had a beautiful tenor voice. I found out that his name was Junho, and that he was Haerin's *oppa* (meaning "older brother"). He was seventeen, a senior at Pusan High School for Boys. I heard Haerin speak proudly of her *oppa* to several church ladies, boasting about his good looks and singing talent.

I heard Haerin tapping her hymn book, demanding my full attention. Standing on her podium, a small step stool that she carefully stored with the hymnals in the closet, she bent forward so that she hung over us, and with her long fingers, she wielded her baton with exaggerated precision. Her blue lace dress with the billowy sleeves made every wave of her arm seem that much more commanding and majestic. Her hair was pulled back, held by a large blue velvet bow perched on her head like a bluebird ready to take flight. I watched her eyes, which at times closed dreamily, and at other times rolled wildly with emotion as she conducted.

When we sang, I often forgot my dislike for her. The songs seemed to transport me to another world. The songs in Latin were my favorites. It was strangely enchanting to be singing in an ancient foreign language, and I felt as if I could suddenly understand those people who had lived so long ago. I attentively followed Haerin's directions and listened carefully to the intermingling of our voices.

Haerin suddenly cocked her head, listened, and brought us to an abrupt stop. "Sookan, you move over here to the center, in front of the organ." Then she looked at her brother Junho and said, "*Oppa*, you move to the center too. Your two voices harmonize well. I think we'll have you do a duet."

Junho, the handsome, quiet tenor smiled at his younger sister's bossy manner, but quickly obliged her and moved next to me. I stood quietly and looked away, as I had nothing official to discuss with Junho. I had never stood so close to a boy other than one of my brothers before, and I tried to contain the smile that kept surfacing to my lips. I could feel myself blushing, and I stared down at my feet, pretending to concentrate on lining them up properly.

As I stood next to him, I could hear how sweetly his mellow voice accompanied mine. Haerin was right; it was better to put us nearer each other. Suddenly, I could hear only our two voices. I had to look around to assure myself that the rest of the choir members were still there. Proud of her arrangement, Haerin signaled for Junho and me to continue singing while the others hummed. Haerin beamed triumphantly as if she had invented something brand new.

Father Lee came over after Mass the following Sunday and complimented her. "Beautifully done! Getting better and better," he said. Then he smiled broadly at Junho and me. My heart pounded, my chest felt tight, my throat burned, and my whole body tingled with a strange blend of exhilaration and embarrassment.

Haerin arranged several duets for Junho and me and we sang many extra verses during Sunday Mass, especially during communion. Although Junho and I didn't know each other and never talked, our singing made us feel close. When we sang alone, I dared to glance at him, and I was glad when he looked back at me and smiled. People moving back to their seats after communion quickly lifted their heads and watched us with admiration. Junho always smiled and nodded to me as if congratulating me on a job well done.

One Sunday, after the last Mass, I was hurrying home as usual, relieved to rest my voice and finally to be away from Haerin. "Sookan, Sookan," a loud, shrill voice called from behind. It was Haerin. "Wait for me. Why do you always dash out? You never talk to me. Let's walk together. We go the same way."

It was true. I always rushed to leave, and I knew I walked right in front of her house. I didn't want to spend any extra time with her, though. Every time I walked by her house, I stayed as far away from it as I could. I kept wishing I could find an alternate road. Browny no longer barked at me; he lazily watched me from his comfortable wooden house shaded by a leafy apricot tree.

Grimacing painfully, I turned and waited for Haerin and tried to think of ways to hide my displeasure. Unlike her soft-spoken brother Junho, she was boisterous, pushy, and arrogant. Why did she want to talk to me today? Did I forget to do something at church? As I waited for her to catch up, I tried to hide my shoebag discreetly at my side. With Haerin, I felt embarrassed that I lived on the refugee mountain and that I had to change shoes for the long climb.

She was breathing heavily when she caught up to me, and I just stared at her in silence, wondering what she wanted. She paused to catch her breath, smoothing her shiny black hair and neatly arranging her lace ribbons. As she shook her wide lace sleeves to make them fall evenly, she filled the air with her lavender perfume. Satisfied that she looked presentable, she said in her piercing voice, "You know, I find you girls from the north intriguing. You've seen so much — the war and all, I mean. Yet all of you are so quiet. None of you talk much about anything, especially you. You always disappear before I'm even ready to leave. Why don't you wait for me? What do you do up there on the mountain?"

When I just stared at her in amazement, she continued. "Sookan, tell me. What was it like to live through a war and escape here to Pusan?"

I sighed and shrugged my shoulders. I didn't know

what to say. How can you explain what war is like to someone who has always lived in a peaceful, beautiful neighborhood, and wears a different fancy lace dress every Sunday? And why her sudden interest in us refugees?

I walked along in silence, hoping we would quickly arrive at Haerin's house. I would hurriedly say goodbye and head for the mountain. I wouldn't change my shoes until she was well out of sight.

But she persisted. "I see your mother working at the information center, and I've seen the notices she posts about refugee families. I like her handwriting; she makes fine strokes. I wish I could write like that. Father Lee told me she used to do some brush painting in Seoul. Was she an artist?"

"I guess so. She used to sketch and paint onto silk screens," I said, trying to keep my answer short without being rude.

"Can I see one of them?" Haerin asked eagerly.

"No. She doesn't have anything with her," I said, exasperated at her innocent curiosity.

"You mean she didn't bring any of her artwork?" she said, raising her eyebrows and wrinkling her nose in disapproval.

I just shook my head in silence. She wouldn't understand that bombs were exploding all around us and enemy tanks were rolling into the city, shooting at anyone and anything. We had to run for our lives. How could she understand that packing valuables and sentimental items never even entered our minds?

After staring at me in silence, she said, "I saw your little brother Inchun the other day. My *oppa* pointed him out to me. I think he's a handsome boy. How big is your family? Mine is very small, just my *oppa* and me and my parents."

"I used to have a large family in Seoul, but not here. At least not for now."

"What do you mean not for now? Are they coming later?"

"I don't know. I hope they will. During the bombing, we got separated. We weren't able to find my father and my three brothers. Maybe they've joined the army and are fighting for us at the front. I don't know." My face flushed, and my head started to pound. "I might see them soon, or I might never see them," I blurted out to stop the tremble in my voice. I didn't want to talk about myself or my family or the war. Afraid of crying in front of Haerin, I started walking even more quickly toward the mountain.

"You two are in such a hurry," called a low, soothing voice from behind us. "Slow down, let me catch up." I wondered if Junho had asked his sister to detain me.

Smiling, he walked toward us. I stood and watched him as he brushed his thick, dark hair away from his face. He was average height, but very well built, with fine square shoulders and a graceful stride. He had a broad forehead, a strong nose, round dark eyes, and a gentle smile. His ears were like those of the Buddha, with long, full earlobes. I knew Mother would take one look at his face and declare him a handsome young man with a kind heart. I clutched my shoebag even more tightly and twirled it nervously.

He stood between Haerin and me, and smiling, he said, "Now, we can walk together."

We walked in silence. I couldn't think of a thing to say. All too soon, we stood in front of their brick wall. For no reason at all, my heart throbbed and my shoulders ached. I jiggled my shoulders and coughed, wishing to be free of this strange discomfort. Junho quietly watched me and smiled. Embarrassed, I wanted to run away, but I stood there, trying to pretend everything was perfectly normal.

He looked up at the mountain that rose before us, and asked, "Sookan, where is your house?"

"Well, you can't really see it from here, but it's way up at the very top," I answered awkwardly.

With his head cocked back, he squinted inquisitively into the sunlight. As I watched his earnest expression, I suddenly wanted to tell him everything about my life up on the mountain. Before I could even think, I heard myself saying, "I can see the whole city of Pusan from my little front yard. Oh, look over there! Do you see the other mountain peak? That is where my shouting poet lives. Every morning he shouts good morning to all of us on the mountain. He is like our alarm clock. In the beginning, people yelled back at him to be quiet, but now everyone is used to it. No one seems to mind anymore, and I love it! What I like best is watching the moon from up there, especially the pale half moon that looks as if someone just sliced it perfectly into two. It's so beautiful, and up on top of the mountain I feel close to the moon, as if I could almost touch it."

I rambled on so quickly that I barely gave myself time to breathe. All my senses were numbed, and I felt as if I had no control over my own tongue. Junho laughed heartily and stared up at the mountain. I flushed with embarrassment, and my face quickly turned the color of ripe raspberries.

When he saw me, he said soothingly, "Oh, please, I think it is wonderful that you're so enthralled with life on the mountain. It must be lovely there where the air is so fresh and clean."

I looked up at the humble shacks cluttering the mountain and felt worse. Staring down at my feet, I twisted the string of my shoebag until it was so tight that my fingers turned blue.

Taking one step closer to me, Junho then said, "You know, Sookan, my sister and I have never been anywhere but Pusan. You have been through so much, and you now know so much more than we ever could. You must feel rich and knowledgeable."

But I felt miserable and small, and wanted to run up the mountain and cry. "*Oppa*, she is not from Seoul," interjected Haerin. "Father Lee told me Sookan originally came from Pyongyang; she was born and raised there. Can you imagine traveling from one end of the Korean peninsula to the other?!"

Poking Junho in the arm, she said, "Go ahead, *Oppa*, ask her about that and ask her about the war, too." Haerin urged Junho on eagerly, as if his asking were the only way to ensure a detailed answer from me.

Haerin was rather pretty when she was being genuine. I suddenly felt a certain affection for her and forgave her ignorance. I untwisted the string of my shoebag and watched my blue fingers regain circulation. Feeling a little calmer, I told her that Pyongyang was not as far north as she thought and that there were many Korean cities farther north than that. Her eyes blinked with excitement and fascination, like a child's. As I talked about Pyongyang, I could feel Junho staring intently at me, and I grew more and more embarrassed.

I finished my sentence and quickly said goodbye, then ran toward the mountain without waiting to hear their responses. I made a point of not changing my shoes until I was halfway up the mountain and was sure that their house was well out of sight.

Chapter Four

At the front of each classroom was a large blackboard supported by the long pieces of wood that Bokhi and I had found by the seashore and had dragged up to the lot one hot muggy day. When we struggled to carry these long poles through the streets, we had no idea they would be used to hold up the shiny blackboards. Eight long benches were neatly arranged in rows, and each bench seated about ten girls. As word spread of the new Ewha School in Pusan, many more former Ewha students who were now refugees came from faraway villages surrounding Pusan. Teacher Yun was sure even more Ewha students were in the area, and she placed a large notice at the refugee center where Mother worked: "Ewha students, all grades, welcome at the new Ewha school."

I was delighted to sit in the first row of the classroom I had helped build. As I listened to Teacher Yun speak of faraway lands, my heart leaped with joy. Those sweltering, hot days of labor seemed a million miles away. Using my lap as my desk, I furiously wrote down everything she said. There was so much to learn and not a minute to lose. The teachers had a few books they had borrowed from the Pusan School teachers, but we students had none, so we had to write everything down.

There were seven teachers in all at our little school. Teacher Yun who taught literature and world history had always been my favorite. Bokhi's favorite, however, was Teacher Lee, our French teacher. Long ago, Bokhi had decided that she wanted to enter the Sorbonne in Paris where Teacher Lee had studied.

We were all most eager to learn. Some of us arrived at dawn, but our teachers were always there even earlier, writing the day's lessons on the blackboard. We studied eagerly, engrossed in our lessons and anxious to catch up with all that we missed over the past several months. Overjoyed to be learning again, I memorized and recited and wrote until my head and hands ached.

During our lunch breaks, Bokhi and I planted some seeds and bulbs in the little yard outside the classroom buildings. Each day we weeded and watered our little garden, waiting for the flowers. Marigolds, wild lilies, daisies, and cosmos soon grew abundantly. Tall sunflower stalks grew from the seeds Teacher Yun had planted, and their sun-baked yellow faces greeted us cheerfully in the morning.

While we were gardening one day, Bokhi told me she was worried about her aunt, who had begun to stare at the front door day and night and mumble, "I can just feel it in my bones. Your uncle is near me. Go get him. Get him over here."

"I don't know if she's going crazy or if she can sense something. What do you think?" Bokhi asked.

When I just shrugged my shoulders, not knowing what to say, Bokhi spoke again. "I put many notes up on the bulletin board about my uncle and my parents, but no one has heard anything about them. During the bombing, we all went running out of the house. My parents and my uncle were right behind my aunt and me, but by the time we reached the main road, we had gotten separated. When I find my uncle, I know I will also find my parents. I'm sure of it," she said, her face flushed with hope.

"I know! I'll tell my mother and she can ask everyone about your uncle and your parents. Maybe someone will come up with good news."

Bokhi suddenly looked pensive, and shook her head sadly. "It's been almost two years since the war began. If they were alive, we probably would have heard something by now. Maybe I'm fooling myself."

"Not necessarily," I replied. "Many people fled Seoul, and they're scattered all over the southern part of the country. Pusan is not the only southern city where refugees came. There are lots of smaller cities and towns. That's what makes it so hard to locate people. Everything is so crazy now, but somehow we'll all get back together, if we wait and trust." My mother had said the same thing to me when I was afraid that I might never see my brothers and my father again.

"Since your aunt feels your uncle might be near, why

don't we concentrate on finding *him* for now. Maybe he's here. Old ladies sometimes feel things, you know. So, what is his name? He is your father's older brother, right?"

"Yes, yes, his name is Changil," said Bokhi, looking less solemn.

"Lee Changil. I'll write a big note tonight for Mother. She will remember and she will keep asking about him whenever she sees a new face in town. She hasn't stopped looking for information about the rest of my family. She says that if we last saw them alive, they must be alive. That's how we should think about it." Bokhi looked a little more cheerful, and I knew she was thinking of the day she would see her parents again.

A few days later, Mother did find someone who had met a man named Lee Changil in a nearby town. Mother sent someone there and confirmed that he was indeed Bokhi's uncle. As her uncle was in poor health, Bokhi and her aunt went to fetch him. The joy of seeing her uncle, however, was eclipsed by his confirmation that Bokhi's parents had died in the bombing. Their house had collapsed and they were trapped. Unable to save them, he had watched them die.

Bokhi did not come to school for several days. Finally, Mother received a note from Bokhi's aunt asking if I could stay with Bokhi for a while at their shack by the seashore. Mother agreed that I should go and try to comfort Bokhi, and get her to go back to school.

For two days and nights, I sat with Bokhi in utter

silence. Her eyes were red and swollen, and her lips were sealed tight. She didn't talk to anyone, not even me. Her aunt and uncle's wrinkled faces wore a look of helplessness, and their eyes seemed to plead with me to bring their sweet niece back to the world of the living.

Bokhi sat in the corner of the room, flipping mindlessly through her French dictionary. She was in her own dark world and seemed not to see anything around her. It scared me to look into her sunken eyes, partly concealed by wisps of tangled hair. Bokhi was always the sensible, orderly, practical one. She didn't believe in wasting time or energy and was always eager to learn and live life to the fullest. I had often thought it strange that she wanted to be a poet. Although she loved poetry, she seldom dawdled, distracted by silly thoughts, as I did. But now, time did not exist for her.

Hoping to bring her back to the world, I asked, "Bokhi, what page are you on now? How many new words have you learned from your dictionary? Here, let's open our French dictionaries to 'M.' You can test me on the meanings and spellings, then I'll test you, just as we always do.

"Come on, Bokhi," I pleaded. "We haven't done this for five days now. Bokhi, talk to me." I felt powerless and silly. I didn't know what I could do to make her feel better.

Bokhi didn't respond. Instead, she got up with her dictionary in her hand and went outside to walk along the seashore. I followed her and, walking beside her, I bravely looped my arm through hers with a smile. She didn't pull away, but she also didn't give my arm her usual squeeze. She didn't seem to care one way or the other. She was somber and aloof, and we just kept walking, passing the rows and rows of gloomy refugee huts. We walked all the way to the jagged black rocks that jutted into the sea. In gloomy silence, we watched the waves crash violently onto the rocks, filling the air with cold, gray mist.

My teeth chattered from the damp cold. Then Bokhi finally spoke. "Now, I am an orphan. I have no parents. Ever since I got separated from my parents, I dreamed of the happy day when I would be reunited with them. That dream kept me going. But now there is nothing for me to dream of. There's nothing to keep me going."

My eyes filled with tears as she spoke. I pulled my arm from hers and hugged myself. I was chilly and tired, and I didn't know what to say. Then, remembering the desperate, pleading faces of her guardians, I said, "Bokhi, don't you see how sad and worried your aunt and uncle are? They are so afraid they have lost you, too."

"Yes, I know I've worried them a great deal. I'll try not to cry and make them sad anymore," she said with determination.

"Bokhi, you're wrong to think you have nothing to dream about and nothing to live for. Your parents now live in your dreams. Now they can dream with you about your future. They would want you to go on studying French and fulfill your dream of going to the Sorbonne.

They will travel with you to France and work with you to become a great poet."

I wasn't sure whether she heard me, but she pulled out her small French dictionary and flipped through the pages intently.

"What word are you looking for?" I asked, relieved to see her lifeless eyes search for something.

"The word for 'sand,' " she said dryly.

"*Sable*. Why? Are you going to write a poem in French about the seashore?"

"No, I wanted to know the word for 'sand castle' in French," she said expressionlessly.

"*Château de sable?*" I said, trying to get a smile out of her.

She didn't even crack a smile but stared down at the black rocks below. Bending suddenly, she fiercely dug her fingers into the wet sand lodged in the crevices of the rock and grabbed a fistful of sand and pebbles. She hurled it angrily into the water. The small pebbles fell loudly into the dark, turgid water.

"There, see how the ocean swallows those little pebbles. We are helpless and insignificant, like the pebbles. The war comes, chases us from our homes, makes us refugees, and then swallows us up along with all our hopes and dreams. We just sink down to the bottom. Only then do we have peace. What's the sense of trying? What's the sense of studying?" She stared at the dark water, taking short breaths as her eyes filled with tears of sadness and helplessness.

"Bokhi, you are wrong," I said firmly. "We can *not* be swallowed up like those little pebbles. We aren't pebbles. We won't just quietly sink to the bottom. We can run, we can fight, and we can work. We are not helpless unless we let ourselves be."

My words were lost in the wind. Staring out at the sea, she said with resignation, "Do you ever feel that we are only building sand castles? Why do so many sad things happen to us? I am afraid the little we have left will be swept away, too. Why bother?" She kicked the rocks. Her hair was flying in her face, and her threadbare blouse hung limply on her thin frame.

"Come on, let's walk toward school. Teacher Yun has been waiting for you. She misses you, and she's been counting on me to get you back." Pulling Bokhi by the arm, I dragged her away from the water and started walking toward our classrooms.

After a few steps, she stopped short and announced, "I don't want to go anywhere. You go to school alone. I want to be by myself and do nothing."

I was ready to give up and cry, but I heard myself shouting at her as I never had before. "You don't even know what you're saying anymore! You're not doing *nothing*, you're doing something terrible. You are making me sad, and your aunt and uncle sad, and you are going to disappoint Teacher Yun. She loves you and wants to see you. I can't go back alone. I will just stand here then, just like you!" I rubbed my eyes to hide the tears filling them.

I longed to see Teacher Yun. I needed to see her broad smile, and her bright and clear eyes. Most of all, I needed to hear her energetic voice. She was always able to cheer me up, and I knew she would know what to do about Bokhi. I knew she could make Bokhi forget about the sand castles and the pebbles. Teacher Yun seemed to have some kind of magical power over her sad students. I pulled Bokhi by the arm, and Bokhi, baffled and shocked at my outburst, slowly followed.

Class was in progress when we arrived, and I could hear the teachers lecturing. When I poked my head into the classroom, Teacher Yun rushed out. She immediately handed me her thick book and a small piece of chalk, saying, "Sookan, take this book and copy the rest of the chapter onto the blackboard for the class." Then she squeezed my hand, and whispered in my ear, "Good work, Sookan. Thanks for bringing her here. She'll be all right. Don't worry." Smiling broadly, she held Bokhi's arm and quickly walked her away.

My arms began to ache from reaching up to the blackboard and my fingertips hurt from clutching the small piece of chalk for so long. As soon as I filled the board and the students had copied what I had written, I had to erase the board and fill it again. My hair and clothes were covered with chalk.

Finally, Teacher Yun returned to the classroom with Bokhi. Bokhi's hair was now neatly braided into two long pigtails that rested on her shoulders. There was a white bow in her hair and she wore a black armband just as

Teacher Yun did. We all knew that Teacher Yun wore the bow and armband to mourn the death of her parents and her brothers. I could almost picture Teacher Yun magically transmitting her strength and determination to her student as she fixed Bokhi's hair, tying the white ribbon in it, and then pinned the thin, black armband to her sleeve.

Teacher Yun had always been able to help me when I was sad about my father and my brothers. For me, it was not so much what she said as the way she looked at me. In her big, sorrowful eyes, I could see how much she cared about me. When she looked deep into my eyes, I felt I *had* to smile, for otherwise I would make her even sadder. When I managed to smile, her face brightened like the sun itself. I wondered if that was what had happened to Bokhi, too. Bokhi seemed more relaxed, and her eyes, though still red and puffy, were bright. I knew then that she and I would soon be testing each other on vocabulary, and gardening, and talking just as we used to.

That evening, I remained at Bokhi's, and we stayed up late copying from Teacher Yun's book all that we had missed over the past few days. Bokhi's hand busily formed small, square letters that looked like those of a typewriter. She reached for the eraser often, making every letter look perfect. I looked at my sweeping handwriting and laughed. I had used twice as much paper as she. The salty smell of the sea seeped through the plywood walls. We could hear the waves roar and crash against the rocks, and in the distance, we could hear the sounds of life in the little refugee dwellings. The candle was burning low and the pale moon was out.

Feeling tired, I looked at Bokhi and said, "Shall we go out and hear the sea roar?"

"Take my shawl. The night air is cold," said her aunt.

Wrapping ourselves together in the shawl, we stood on the shore and inhaled the chilly, salty air, and listened to the waves break. I rested my head on Bokhi's shoulder. I was happy to have her back and grateful to Teacher Yun.

"I'm glad you dragged me back to Teacher Yun today, Sookan," she said quietly. "She made me realize that my parents can still be with me in my mind and heart. I was so angry and sad, I just couldn't believe that before. Teacher Yun made me see that they will always be there watching over me and taking care of me. I want them to be proud of me in every way. I'll try not to be so sad, because I don't want to bring more sadness to all the people who love me. I hope that I can be as strong and as inspiring as Teacher Yun someday, and help someone else as she helped me."

"You know, when I grow up, I want to be a teacher, just like Teacher Yun," I said.

Squeezing my hand, she said, "I thought you wanted to be a writer and a nun."

"Well, I can be all of those."

Bokhi smiled and squeezed my hand again.

Chapter Five

The next evening, I headed back home, eager to see Mother and Inchun, and looking forward just to being up on top of the mountain. I missed the friendly voice of the shouting poet.

As I climbed, I suddenly realized that during the last few months, while I had been busy rushing to and from school, the mountain had undergone a transformation. How could I have failed to notice? The mountain was not so difficult to climb as it used to be. The path up the hill had become worn and smooth from constant use. In some of the steep areas that were difficult to climb, people had dug little footholds that made it more like climbing a ladder. Now there were even some plants and shrubs growing along the path, which kept the dry and rocky mountain soil from eroding.

People had all tried to make their little huts more homey by creating their own unique gardens. The once identical shacks all looked different now, each bearing the creative stamp of its residents. Wild lilies, daisies, and azaleas bloomed in some front yards. One hut had nothing but tall yellow sunflowers, while another had morning glories scaling the walls and climbing the roof. Another had rows of tin cans blossoming with pansies and marigolds neatly arranged around the perimeter of the house. It was as if each little house were furiously competing to be the prettiest, most cheerful one on the mountain.

When I arrived home, I was greeted by tall sunflowers, their heads heavy with ripening seeds. I knew Mother was waiting to harvest these seeds. My favorite flower, the wild cosmos, surrounded our little shack, and morning glory vines climbed the larger beams.

I had missed the fresh mountain air and my spectacular view of Pusan. I heard laughter ringing through the mountains, and I looked down at the long line of women and children standing at the well. Children were laughing and shouting, mock fighting with their buckets. Their mothers, while yelling at them to be still, laughed and talked among themselves as they waited in line.

That night I talked to Mother until the thin sliver of moon rose high over the mountaintop. Inchun plugged his ears with a piece of cotton and went to sleep. He grimaced at my endless chatter about Bokhi and Teacher Yun.

The next morning I sprang out of bed. The sun was high in the sky already. Had I overslept, I wondered? Was I late for choir practice? Inchun, who was reading a book, lifted his head and said teasingly, "Afraid your choir conductor will embarrass you?"

"No, I just don't like to be late for anything. I meant to be up early."

I looked around, feeling that something was not quite right on the mountain. Could it have been because I had been away and had gotten used to the seashore? Perhaps I just felt strange because I had overslept. I couldn't tell what was wrong. So, I went outside and looked over at the other mountain peak where the shouting poet always stood. I ran back in and said, "Inchun, did you hear the shouting poet this morning? I didn't hear him. I've never slept through his morning wake-up call. Did he shout this morning?"

Instead of answering me, Inchun slid down under his blanket. Then he stared intently at his science book as if he were trying to solve a very difficult question. He began to whistle while I glared at him and waited for an answer. I knew something was wrong. Inchun often teased me, but he was never rude; he never just ignored me like that. I ran to the kitchen.

"Mother, did you hear the shouting poet this morning?"

She didn't answer me either. She methodically checked the rice to see if it was done.

"Mother, did you hear him yesterday? Did something happen to him?"

In silence, she wiped her hand on her white apron and went around to the back of the house. Letting out a long, weighty sigh, she said, "Sookan, come and sit down next to me.

"I should have told you yesterday when you returned, but I didn't have the heart to bring it up. And you were busy telling me about Bokhi. I thought you needed some time after seeing your friend through that difficult period."

I knew my shouting poet had died. He wasn't ill and he hadn't just moved away or gone somewhere for a couple of days. Mother's somber expression said it all.

"When did he die, Mother? When? How did it happen?" I wanted to know. My head was pounding and I felt a shooting pain in my eyes. I felt like stomping on the ground and screaming. Why couldn't I stop these sad and horrible things from happening all around me? What else would happen to me and the people I loved?

"Tell me, Mother, tell me everything!" I yelled. "Tell me how he died and when."

Mother sighed. "The day after you left for Bokhi's house, he shouted as usual, but after that, we didn't hear him anymore. At the water line, I learned that after he shouted that morning, he doubled over in pain. He had an advanced case of tuberculosis and he spat blood each morning after shouting his greeting. The physician at the health center apparently told him not to be out in the cold mountain air shouting in the morning, but he wouldn't stop. He even shouted the morning he died. They say he was originally from Kwangwon province and he was indeed quite a well-known poet. When the war broke out, he lost all his family and escaped here alone.

"Although no one returned his morning greeting, we all felt the loss. Everyone gave money to buy a tombstone in his honor. I knew you would be glad to know how much people cared."

I listened in silence, feeling the sadness and anger welling up inside me. Why did he have to leave us? Why hadn't anyone shouted back to him to let him know that he was appreciated while he was alive? What good was a tombstone now that he was dead? Why had I never climbed that other mountain to see him? All sorts of thoughts went through my mind as I stared at the empty mountaintop on the other side.

"I heard he was in pain much of the time, Sookan. Now he is free of that pain," Mother said, trying to comfort me. But it didn't help at all. I still sat there, numb and engulfed by sadness.

Mother hugged me and stroked my hair. "Sookan, we can go visit his grave. We will read what was written on his tombstone. Then we can plant some seeds and take some of the seashells you collected and decorate the grave."

Wiping the tears from my cheeks, I nodded. "I want to take some sand and mix it with the soil, too, so that the plants will grow fast and flower soon," I mumbled.

"Yes, we will do all of that early tomorrow. Today I still have too much work to get finished," Mother said.

I didn't go to choir practice that day. On Sunday, Mother and I went to Mass at dawn, and then we started up the poet's mountain. This mountain was even higher

49

than ours, and the poet's grave was at the very top. When we arrived, we saw withered roses, daisies, and cosmos covering the grave.

A smooth, gray stone slab stood in front of the mound of earth and read, "Baik Rin, 1899–1952. May he rest in peace in God's love. May he shout his morning greeting to us each day in our dreams. From his fellow mountain refugees." Each letter was deeply and clearly chiseled into the cold gray stone. I traced each letter with my index finger, one by one.

How ironic that his name was Baik Rin, meaning "White Giraffe." I thought that giraffes did not make any sounds, yet this was the name of my shouting poet. The giraffe was my favorite animal and I had once read that giraffes like to eat the tender spring leaves of the acacia trees as they are filled with morning dew. I promised myself that someday I would come up here again and plant some acacia saplings around his grave. I imagined a tall, graceful white giraffe happily feeding on a grove of acacia trees here at the top of the mountain.

"White giraffe, white giraffe," I kept mumbling to myself, wondering why these words sounded so familiar to me. Suddenly I remembered the story of the white giraffe that my grandfather used to tell me when I was very little. I had not thought of that story for a long time. Grandfather said that ages ago, there was a kindhearted scholar who saw a white giraffe in the forest. He was overwhelmed by its grace and beauty, but he was frightened for it. Without the natural camouflage of an ordinary giraffe, this white giraffe looked very vulnerable and helpless. The hunters and curious villagers would surely spot this delicate, precious creature and scare it or harm it. So the scholar draped himself in a long white cape, wore a tall white hat, and strolled through the forest every morning while the giraffe grazed on the leaves of the tall trees. When the hunters and villagers saw the mysterious white figure walking among the green trees, they simply said, "Oh, that eccentric scholar must be taking a walk again." And they always stayed far away from that part of the forest.

I could not recall the rest, but I remembered how enchanted I had been with this story. Maybe that was why I had always been so fond of giraffes.

"Come on, Sookan," Mother said. "Sprinkle some sand over the seeds I planted and then cover the sand gently with red mud. Why not place the seashells around this little area so that people won't step on it?" I busily covered and packed the seeds so that they would grow and bloom for the shouting poet.

"Good," said Mother. "I see rain clouds hanging low over the mountains. The rain will be good for the seeds, and soon flowers will blossom and grace the poet's grave. Come. Now we must hurry home." Without looking back, I followed Mother down the mountain in silence and thought of the shouting poet in his white T-shirt with his head tilted back and his hands cupped around his mouth. I could almost hear his voice echoing through the mountains.

Chapter Six

Pelted by the rapid fire of raindrops, the tin roofs emitted their deafening cries. "Plank! Plank! Plank-plank-plank-plank! Plank!" I was glad that it was raining so hard. I could not bear to see the sun shine today. I wanted the whole world to weep for my shouting poet.

I went outside and stood in the middle of my dirt yard. My feet sank into the red mud, which was quickly washed away by the torrents of rain. I kept thinking of the poet. Why did he have to die? Didn't he know that I needed him? I wished I had seen him up close just once. The rain streamed down my face, carrying my salty tears with it. Too many things kept changing in my life and I wondered what else would be taken from me. I couldn't be sure of what tomorrow would bring. I was afraid. Cold and drenched, I just stood there in the rain, trembling with fear and sadness.

Mother ordered me to come inside. Standing by the door, I continued to gaze outside and watch the rain fall. My poet's voice still rang in my ears when I looked at his mountain. Behind this veil of rain, I felt I could see his thin, gray figure waving to me. He was telling me he would shout his morning greeting to me in my dreams, just as they had written on his tombstone. Too tired to cry anymore, I remained standing by the door, looking down the mountain.

A man was walking up the muddy path. Hunched over, with his head bent to watch his next step, he seemed to be heading right for our house. I squinted to see who it was. As he drew closer, he paused, looking right and left. He then looked straight up at our shack. I could see him better. It was Junho.

My heart stopped. What was he doing here? Why was he coming up here in such bad weather? Was he coming to see me? Would Mother let him? It was not permitted for a boy to come visit a girl unless they were engaged. What was I to do? My head ached from trying to think so fast, but my heart raced with excitement. I couldn't help thinking how wonderful it would be! I could really talk to him, ask him all sorts of questions, and tell him everything I had always wanted to. Was Haerin coming too? I looked down the road and didn't see anyone behind him.

As he drew closer, I saw that his shoes and the bottom of his slacks were caked with red mud. Even his coat sleeves were red and muddied; he must have fallen several times. It must have been quite a climb for him in this downpour. Not knowing what to do, I just watched him draw closer and closer.

As he came to the door, Mother saw him and jumped up. "My stars! Junho? What brings you here on such a treacherous day? You must come in and dry out. Hurry, Sookan! Run, get a big towel."

Blushing awkwardly, he said, "Oh, thank you. I'm sorry to intrude. I need not trouble you. I just came to give this to you." He carefully pulled out a small, well-wrapped package from inside his raincoat. "Father Lee asked me to bring this piece of white silk for you to paint on."

A few months earlier, a wealthy Pusan resident had wanted a special painting for a wedding cushion, and Father Lee had told him about Mother. When people saw how beautiful and delicate her silk screen paintings were, many began asking Father Lee to ask Mother to paint for them. Father Lee always made sure that Mother was paid and that the paint and the silk were supplied for her.

"Thank you," Mother said to Junho as she took the package. She was pleased, for she loved to paint, and we always needed the money. "But it is so far for you to have come," she added. "Come in. You must at least have a cup of tea before you venture downhill."

I quickly nodded with enthusiasm, but stopped short, afraid Mother would see how inappropriately pleased I was at the prospect of his staying for tea. It was clever of Junho to have had such an appropriate excuse for coming to see me. And I was glad that Inchun happened to be out on a science field trip, for he would have given me disapproving stares all through Junho's visit.

Junho sat by the door and I sat on the opposite side of

the room. In silence, he looked around the tiny room that served as both our living room and bedroom. The blankets were neatly rolled up in one corner, and one small wooden bookcase stood in the opposite corner. A small sketch of a Buddhist temple done on a piece of yellowed rice paper caught his eye. I saw him carefully study the delicate pine branches and the three small birds flying around the Buddhist temple.

"What a beautiful sketch. Is this your Mother's work?"

"Well, this is just doodling for her. Here she doesn't have large silk canvases, brushes of all sizes, and fine paint as she used to in Seoul. In Seoul, we had many large, beautiful paintings that Mother had done."

Junho fell quiet and stared down at the shiny floor. "I didn't exactly tell your mother the truth."

"What do you mean?" I asked.

"Well, Father Lee didn't exactly ask me to come up here. After Mass, we talked about you and how you had been absent from choir practice yesterday and from all four Masses today. He mentioned that he had planned to give you a package to take home to your mother. I quickly offered to deliver it. It seemed like a good excuse to come and see you." He smiled.

"Where were you yesterday and today?" he then asked. "Were you sick?"

"No, I wasn't sick. I was just too sad. My shouting poet died and I just couldn't sing. Mother and I went to dawn Mass and then went to visit his grave this morning, and it took several hours."

His soft dark eyes intently studied my face, and he fell silent. We heard Mother preparing our tea, and I smelled something delicious. It smelled like honey and cinnamon, which we had not had for a very long time.

Junho, who had been looking at my puffy eyes, said softly, "You know, your shouting poet is still alive in many people's hearts. Today Father Lee was asked by many to say a special Mass for the shouting poet. You mustn't cry and grieve for him. He doesn't need the normal kind of grieving. He is above all that."

"I know what you mean," I said, mustering a smile. "I cried for a while, but then I realized he was in my heart and I decided that he would live on. I'm happy that we will be having a Mass for him."

Junho smiled, and reached inside his chest pocket. Placing a thin paperback in front of me, he said, "Here, this is for you. This is what I really came for. You once mentioned how much you love the half moon, and when I saw this book, I thought of you."

"*Half Moon: a book of poetry by foreign poets,*" I read aloud.

The pale blue book jacket had a half moon poised over a mountain top. I smiled as I flipped through the pages. There were poems by Shelley, Keats, Blake, Gide, Longfellow, and Tagore, my favorite of them all. I couldn't utter a word. My head was spinning and my heart was pounding. I had never had a boy come visit and bring me presents. I held the book close to my heart, hoping to silence the thumping I heard within. I stared at the book again, pretending to read, but the small print just looked like millions of ants rushing about their daily duties.

I didn't know how to thank him. If it were Bokhi, I would give her a hug, and we would lean our heads together and start to read aloud, or we would go for a long walk with our pinkies hooked together and pledge our eternal friendship for the umpteenth time. This was perfectly acceptable to do with a girlfriend, but with Junho, everything was forbidden. So I sat opposite him and just flipped through the pages aimlessly, trying to bring the words into focus.

"Good, I am glad you like it. When you finish reading it, let me know which poem is your favorite. Did you notice my inscription on the front page?"

I had been so excited that it hadn't even occurred to me to look. I quickly opened to the first page. It read, "To Sookan, a lover of poetry and of the half moon. From your everlasting friend Junho. 1952, Pusan."

Everlasting, everlasting . . . What a comforting word! Just the word I needed to hear when everything I loved seemed to be slipping away from me. An everlasting friend. I savored the sound and repeated it over and over again in my mind as I held the book tight.

I felt so happy that all my nervousness melted away. I hugged the thin book as if it were the dearest thing I had ever owned and said with excitement, "Oh, Junho, thank you, thank you so much. Everlasting friend, how wonderful, how wonderful!"

For a second, Junho's face turned crimson with embarrassment at my sudden effusiveness, but soon a broad smile spread across his face and his eyes twinkled. He looked so handsome that I forgot my manners and just stared at him. It was fortunate that Mother came in with the tea tray before I made a fool of myself.

The aroma of ginger tea filled the room. Then I saw the paper-thin rice biscuits coated with honey, sprinkled with cinnamon, and dotted with white pine nuts. I hadn't seen such delicacies since I had left Seoul. I didn't even know Mother had these ingredients here and was amazed at how she always managed to do just the right thing. Later, I learned that when Mother heard about the shouting poet's death, she had started to prepare these biscuits to comfort me. I felt as though the spirit of my shouting poet was helping to bring my friendship with Junho into reality.

Mother looked very happy to be drinking tea with us. I could almost hear her thinking, "How nice to have a young man in the house. He is the same age as my third son."

But suddenly, Mother's face turned somber, and she looked as if she were about to cry. Taking a deep breath, she got up, and said, "Junho, you must excuse me. I must get my painting started. It is a small canvas, but small things seem to take even more care and time. It is still raining very hard, so why don't you stay and enjoy your tea. It is too dangerous to go downhill in this weather."

Junho, trying to contain the smile spreading across his

face, thanked my mother politely. He looked out at the dark sky gratefully. Were it not for the rain, Junho would have felt compelled to get up and say goodbye. I hoped that the rain would not stop for a long time. As I gazed down at the book he had given me, I wished I had something to give him in return to remember the day by. But I had nothing. I looked around the empty room in despair. If we were in Seoul, I would simply pick one of my favorite books from my tall bookcase and give it to him. With a sigh of frustration, I stared at the sad little bookcase that held my three used notebooks and Inchun's rock collection.

"Is that a picture of your dog?" Junho asked, looking at the pencil sketch of Luxy that rested on top of the bookcase. "You must miss it very much. Please, don't look so sad."

"Oh, that," I said, flustered and surprised. "Yes, that's my boxer, Luxy." I missed my dog, but I hadn't talked about her with anyone since we left Seoul, except once with my mother when she first drew that picture for me. Inchun and I never talked of Luxy either. But I knew all three of us thought of her often and missed her. I frequently thought of how Luxy used to wait eagerly at the top of the stone steps in front of our house for me to come home from school. Then, at night, she would sleep at the foot of my bed. But I never talked of Luxy, for I was afraid that people might think I was childish and insensitive to mourn the loss of my dog when so many people were dead or missing. Junho was different, though. He wore a look of anguish as he studied my face, almost reading my thoughts, and sharing my sadness.

"I like the sketch Mother did. She really captured Luxy's personality. She was a ferocious-looking boxer, but at the same time she was so gentle and intelligent. She always sat up straight like that, showing off her handsome figure. Those big brown eyes studied everything that went on. No one ever had to order her around. She somehow always knew just what to do." I rambled on as I thought of our happy days in Seoul. "She was so intelligent, she even delivered the right magazines to the right readers. She carried *Time* magazine to Jaechun, the newspaper to my father, and science magazines to Inchun. She was an amazing dog. She had us all convinced that she understood what we were saying, and sometimes even what we were thinking."

"She is the best-looking boxer I ever saw," said Junho, smiling warmly.

I stared at Luxy's picture, and I imagined how scared she must have felt when we all abandoned her. Suddenly the acrid smell of bombs and sweeping fires filled my lungs, and the sound of sirens and planes flying low overhead buzzed in my ears. My mind raced back to that horrible day in late June when the dark airplanes roared through the skies and dropped a shower of dark, egg-shaped bombs from their bellies. The bombs had exploded violently, erupting into a mass of red flames that rose into clouds of heavy black smoke.

I shook my head and swallowed hard to make sure that I did *not* have the gritty taste of ash in my mouth.

"What is it, Sookan? What are you thinking about?" Junho said, looking very concerned.

"Oh, Junho, I was just remembering the first bombing of Seoul. It was horrible. The city was transformed into a burning Hell before my eyes. All I could do was stand by the window and watch the bombs explode. Hyun-chun, my third brother, came rushing into my room, shouting, 'There you are! Come on. Those planes will be right on top of us next. Let's go.' "

"Did you all get out safely?" Junho asked anxiously, his dark eyes staring at me.

"Oh, yes. We put thick blankets over our heads and joined the throngs of people headed up Namsan Mountain. We stayed up on the mountain all night and watched the bombs erupt into flames in the city below. We heard buildings crumble, trees crack, and then, screams of death. As we were sitting there, I realized my brother Jaechun was holding a large bundle in his arms, which he rocked back and forth like a baby. I instantly realized it was Luxy wrapped in that bundle. I had been so frightened, I hadn't even thought of Luxy until I saw Jaechun holding her. While I had stood by my window in shock watching the bombs fall, Mother had been wrapping up Luxy. It was a good thing that Luxy was bundled up to look like an infant, for other people on the mountain would have been afraid if they knew a dog was with

61

them. They would have panicked, fearing that a dog would go crazy with the noise and the crowds and might bite them."

"You mean Luxy sat through the bombing without making a sound?" Junho asked incredulously.

"Oh, no! Jaechun said she moaned and whimpered a lot. But Luxy's ears were well covered with rubber shoes and pillows, and even her eyes were covered. Mother left only Luxy's nose exposed so that she could breathe. Jaechun thinks it was the smell of the bombs that bothered Luxy most."

"How long were you on the hill?"

"All night long. The bombing finally stopped at dawn, and we began making our way back home. We found our house half bombed and smoldering. We were hungry, and exhausted, and didn't know what we would do next. We sat on the stoop and started to unwrap poor Luxy. When we uncovered her, she gave such a loud, joyous bark. She shook her body vigorously and started jumping and running around the yard, celebrating her freedom. She made us laugh and forget that we were sitting in the middle of a bombed city."

Junho's face brightened. "I'm glad everyone was all right. Luxy was lucky to be so well loved and cared for."

"Well, I don't know where she is now. Things got worse. About six months after that, we had to leave Seoul. I left her all alone. I don't know what happened to her. When the North Korean Communists and Communist Chinese came in January, they were shooting everyone in sight. There were more bombs, and we had to run and follow the retreating South Korean and U.N. soldiers going south. It was chaos, and Mother, Inchun and I were separated from my father and my three older brothers. The three of us, along with thousands of other refugees, walked the whole day in the bitter cold snow to Inchon harbor. I was terribly cold and scared. My feet were frozen, but I didn't even realize it until we were aboard a big gray ship headed for Pusan. It was only once we were on the ship that I even thought of my Luxy. Can you believe it? I felt so guilty and ashamed that I never mentioned Luxy to Mother or to Inchun.

"Mother must have known how much it bothered me, because she drew this sketch for me. Each time I see a dog or hear a dog bark, I feel guilty that I did not love Luxy enough to save her; she, my dog, who depended on me. I had thought only of myself. Mother tried to make me feel better by saying it couldn't be helped, that it was too crazy and too horrible. But I still can't help feeling guilty and sad whenever I think of it."

Junho listened intently, with his hands folded tightly in his lap. "You couldn't have walked with her in that cold snow. She may still be alive in Seoul. You shouldn't feel bad." He then took a deep breath and asked with concern, "Do you have any idea of what happened to your father and brothers?"

"I don't know. Mother thinks they probably joined the army. I saw many young men hopping onto the army trucks that drove by. The streets were so crowded with people and with retreating soldiers that I didn't even see my father and brothers after we left the house. We were pushed along by the crowds all the way to Inchon harbor. We thought we might find them here in Pusan, but we still have had no news of them."

Junho was silent for a while. Then he looked up and said, "Well, maybe they did join the army and are busy protecting us. Maybe you'll hear from them soon, and they'll join you here. I'm so sad that you have suffered so much, Sookan. But life is strange, isn't it? As awful as the war is, it *is* because of the war that we're sitting here talking together now. The war brought us our friendship, which is something we shall keep forever." He looked at me expectantly.

I nodded in silence, overwhelmed by a surge of strange, new feelings.

I heard Junho take a deep breath and clear his throat. With tremendous gravity, he said, "I've been meaning to ask you something. Can you tell me what you want to do when you finish Ewha High School?"

"Oh, I know exactly what I want to do. I'm going to America to study history," I said with confidence. "Then, I'll come back to Seoul and join my sister Theresa in the convent. She often tells me how happy she is helping the less fortunate. She is waiting for me to join her. And I want to teach and write as well. There's so much I want to do."

"But why America? It's so far away. You can study

64

history at Korean universities, too, you know," he responded incredulously. "And do you really want to be a nun?"

"Yes, I'm positive — after I get my history degree in America, that is. I know I could study history here, but ever since I was little I've wanted to meet people beyond the Pacific Ocean. I want to know about them, and I want them to know about me. I want to see what it's like there. But most of all, I want to study history there.

"I often wonder what Americans think about a small country like Korea. Our peninsula is so tiny and yet it is constantly being occupied or fought over. My family and I ran away from the Russians in Pyongyang; then, once we settled in Seoul and were living a normal, happy life, we were driven away by the North Koreans and Communist Chinese. I don't understand how history and politics work, and maybe if I study in America, I will understand better."

Junho knit his brow as he listened. "Well, I still think America is too far to go. But if that is your dream, I suppose you should follow it. You sound as if you have given a lot of thought to the matter."

He seemed puzzled and disturbed, and fell silent. I watched his somber expression and could almost see him ruminating on our conversation. Having lived in Pusan all his life, I wondered if he could understand a girl's desire to go so far away. I saw him trying to form a smile to mask his confusion.

"Well, it's still a long time before I even graduate from Ewha High School," I said. "What about you? Do you know what you want to be?"

"I know what I *have* to be. My parents expect me to go to Pusan College this coming spring and then on to Pusan Medical School. I am expected to open an office right next to my father's. I am to be the town doctor, just like my father and his father before him. I must not break the Min family tradition." He stared gloomily at his folded hands.

"You could sing for your patients to ease their pain. You could be the first great singing doctor," I said cheerfully, not quite knowing the right response.

Junho's face brightened at the thought, but then he sighed deeply. "I am more interested in philosophy. I love reading the works of the great philosophers, but my parents think it's a waste of time. They wish I would pore over the medical books we have at home instead. I've just finished reading a book on Thomas Aquinas, and Father Lee said he would be happy to discuss it, if I wanted to. Maybe I will go see him."

"Sookan, look, look at the beautiful rainbow!" Mother exclaimed as she came back into the room. Junho and I looked out. I hadn't even realized that the rain had stopped. A brilliant rainbow shimmered gloriously in the western sky. But for the first time I was not happy to see such a magnificent sight.

Junho got up, took his hat and coat, and quietly mumbled to me, "I must be going. I have no business staying now."

I didn't say anything. I just stood up beside him and stared out at the blue-gray evening sky, wishing it would suddenly start to pour again. There was so much more that I wanted to talk about with Junho, but I knew he couldn't stay any longer.

I saw Mother watching, waiting expectantly for him to go. I couldn't blame her. I knew what she must have been thinking. "It isn't proper for him to stay now. What will people think? They will say that I am not raising my daughter properly because she has no father and no elder brothers around. Besides, I might give Sookan the wrong impression. She should know that it isn't proper for her to chat the whole afternoon away with a young man." For once I wished Mother would forget all about tradition and the neighbors and just let me talk to Junho a little longer.

"Last week, I went with my father to assist some of the army medical officers," Junho said, looking at Mother. "They were saying that a truce is being negotiated. They said that it should not be too long before people can return to their homes in Seoul. You must be looking forward to going home."

"Well, it is our home and we should go back when we can. I hope my sons and my husband will be there waiting for us. Our house, however, will probably be no more than a heap of rubble." She sighed pensively. "I don't know what we will find there, but we have to go back and face our fate and start picking up the pieces again."

Shaking her head with exasperation, Mother continued, "Well, who knows how long it will really be before we can go home again. This war has been such a seesaw. The Communists seized Seoul, the U.N. and South Korean forces recaptured Seoul, then the Communist Chinese and the North Communists seized Seoul again. We have no control over our own destiny. The Japanese occupied Korea for decades, and now there are the Communist Chinese, and, of course, the tricky Russians, working behind the scenes with the North Communists."

Junho nodded with understanding.

"Oh, Junho, here I am keeping you even longer," Mother said, throwing her hands in the air. "You have a long way to go. Thank you for coming up."

Junho bowed deeply to Mother, nodded goodbye to me, and left to battle the slippery mountain. Mother pensively watched him go down the hill. I had thought she might ask him to stay for dinner. But I knew I was being silly. That was out of the question.

Mother stared out into the distance, and I knew she was thinking of the days before the war, when she would listen to my father and brothers heatedly discuss international politics late into the night. Proud of her smart sons and husband, Mother would busily provide drinks and hot food to fuel their discussions. Meanwhile, she would listen to as much of their conversation as she could, soaking up all the information. I remembered how

I used to wish I could sit and listen without having to get up to help Mother in the kitchen. But Mother always seemed happy refilling their cups and plates, and watching them gobble up the food that had taken her all day to prepare.

I watched Junho grow smaller and smaller as he walked down the hill, until he finally disappeared from sight. I felt lonely all of a sudden, and I felt like running after him yelling, "Stop, stop! Wait for me. I'll walk you down." But instead, I stood rigid, with my lips pressed tight, and I stared down at the shacks below.

"It was nice to have him visit. He will make a fine doctor," Mother said as she glanced over at me.

I thought about the armistice. Just as I had gotten used to life here on refugee mountain, had started school again and had found an everlasting friend, I would have to go back. But back to what? I was too tired to think about it all. I plopped down on the little wooden ledge and watched the night seize the sky. I heard Inchun whistling as he returned home.

Chapter Seven

A rickety old bus waited outside the church to take the choir members on a picnic as a group of women fluttered about loading the bus with baskets of food and drink. To thank us for our singing, the women from the church had rented the bus and packed all our favorite picnic foods. Exhausted, but excited for us, they waved goodbye. Knowing how much trouble they had gone to, I felt as if I were sitting in the most beautiful chariot laden with the most exquisite delicacies.

The boys sat on the right side of the bus and the girls on the left. As expected, Haerin, who was sitting at the very front, turned and knelt on her seat, pulled her baton from her bag, and like a magician with a wand, waved her baton to make the music begin. We started somewhat reluctantly, but soon we all broke into song.

Moving my mouth perfunctorily, I stared out the small, dusty window. Cows grazed lazily, a few lifting their heads to look at the speeding bus. The modest country farmhouses, trees, and animals all formed part of the moving picture I watched through the window. I looked over at Junho and saw that he, too, was gazing out the window deep in reverie.

When the bus finally came to a stop, we stepped out onto a large, open field of wildflowers. Giant dragonflies, with their transparent wings, flew in front of us in pairs. Tiger butterflies flew high and low, boasting bold black and yellow patterns emblazoned on their wings. We walked through the fields toward a clearing, lined with rows of clean army barracks, identical in every way. Off to the side, at the end of a wide concrete-paved walk, was an imposing, red-brick building that had been the army headquarters. Flanking the entrance to this building were two tall poplar trees, standing at attention. Everything exuded a sense of orderliness. Handsome soldiers, in their well-pressed uniforms and spit-shined shoes, marched by, saluting when they passed each other, or when their officers sped by in Jeeps. The birds, however, seemed oblivious and chirped noisily as they flew past the army headquarters toward the field of wildflowers. I could see why the church ladies had chosen this as the site for our picnic. The disciplined perfection of the army base against the colorful abandon of the fields created a strangely comforting and beautiful atmosphere.

Led by Father Lee, we strolled around the grounds. Junho took off his jacket, slung it over his shoulder, and lagged behind, humming. Observing every move her *oppa* made, Haerin, too, slowed down to keep him company. I heard Junho say, "Haerin, maybe this is a good time for Sookan and me to practice our duets."

Pulling my sleeve, Haerin said, "Sookan, walk with us. Let's sing."

Haerin was single-minded when it came to her choir, and Junho had cleverly seized the opportunity to get us together. I saw a broad smile spread across his face as I joined them. Walking backwards so that she could face us, Haerin waved her arms, and as we sang, she raised her eyebrows up and down and formed her mouth into little oh's and ah's to prompt us. Our songs carried in the crisp air, and even the disciplined soldiers smiled with approval as they passed us.

The choir started breaking up into several groups to tour the exhibits at the army headquarters. But Junho, Haerin, and I headed for the field where the wildflowers and tall grass grew. I was thankful for Haerin's company. Were it not for her presence, Junho and I wouldn't have been able to walk, talk, and sing together. It wouldn't have been proper for us to walk alone together unless we were engaged, and even then, we would have had to be chaperoned by a family member for propriety's sake. With Haerin along, however, nothing seemed unusual, and I felt assured that we would not attract disapproving stares.

As we walked farther into the overgrown field, we saw a cluster of unusually large, bright yellow lilies swaying in the wind. "Oh, look, *Oppa*! Those are the yellowest lilies I've ever seen! Go and pick some for me!"

"Haerin, they will soon wilt in your warm hands," he said disapprovingly.

Haerin pouted and stormed ahead, stomping her feet. But when Junho broke into the Pusan High School song, she ran back, reclaimed her place next to her older brother, and joined him mid-verse. Haerin's childish behavior amused me, and I saw how intensely she loved her brother.

When the bus dropped us off back at the church that evening, Junho dashed upstairs and brought back two hymnals.

"Why are you going to take them home, *Oppa?*" Haerin asked, looking puzzled.

"Well, I don't think I know all the words to the *Gloria*," he said earnestly. "This book's version seems a bit different from those we have at home. If Sookan and I are to sing a duet next Sunday, we'd better read through it carefully."

I was just about to say, "I know all the words. I don't need to take it with me." But something in Junho's eyes and in the way he tightly clutched the books told me that it was better to keep quiet.

We headed home, chatting and singing as usual, with Haerin walking between us. Once in a while, when we thought Haerin wasn't looking, we'd share a brief glance. All too soon, we arrived in front of Junho's house at the foot of the mountain.

Handing me one of the two hymnals, he said with great formality, "Here, Sookan, you had better take one and go over the text again. It is on page one thirty-five. Be careful, as some of the pages are falling out."

I tried to think of something to say so that we could linger and talk a bit more, but Haerin tugged at his sleeve. "Come on, *Oppa*. Mommy will be wondering where we are." Junho wore a strange smile of resignation, and followed his sister in silence, like a docile bear.

I clutched the book tightly and rushed up the mountain, wondering why all the fuss about the *Gloria*. When I arrived at my favorite spot near the well, I sat on a small rock and opened to page 135. A thin white envelope fell onto my lap. Excited, I stared at the pristine white envelope. There was nothing written on it, but it had to be for me. A letter to me from Junho! I had never received a letter from a boy before, and all the excuses and secrecy made this letter all the more precious and special.

I broke the tight seal. A short note read, "Sookan, soon you will be returning to your home in Seoul. The negotiations seem to be winding down and it looks as though they will be signing an armistice agreement. Before you leave Pusan, I would like you to meet me at the photo studio — you've passed it several times — the one with the silly sign, 'Beautiful Pictures, Every Time.' Please come! I will be waiting, Friday at 4 P.M. Junho."

I read the letter over and over again. Each time I read it, my heart raced with excitement and delight. His handwriting was clear and strong. I could almost see his gentle, dark eyes imploring me to come.

I knew where the studio was. It was on my way home from Ewha. Many times I had wondered about that place.

When might Junho have seen me passing the studio? I had never seen him in that part of town. Did he sometimes follow me as I walked home from school? Maybe he just happened to be passing by and saw me. What a wonderful idea to have our picture taken together! Why hadn't I thought of it? How sweet of him to arrange it all so cleverly. I would surely go meet him there.

I read the note again, very slowly this time. *I must calm down*, I thought. *I can't go. I mustn't.* What was the matter with me? Had I gone insane? Only engaged couples could have their pictures taken together. A marriage needs to have been agreed upon by the families to justify taking a picture together. It's not as if he were my brother or first cousin. Junho should know all this. What could be the matter with him? Had he lost his senses? How could he ask me to do such a rebellious thing and expect me to show up? Does he think that I am so wild and impetuous that I would do such a thing just because he asked? Doesn't he know that I would disgrace myself and my family? He must know my mother would never allow such a thing! I shook my head in determination. I would not go! I could not! That was it. I wanted to crumble the note and stick it back into the book as if it didn't matter.

But Junho was so special to me. And I would soon be leaving Pusan. We would probably never see each other again. I would certainly love to have a photo to remember him by. Maybe I could ask Mother for permission for this special souvenir. But I knew she would forbid it. It was simply out of the question. Such things were never done. "Such a disgrace. Disgrace!" I shouted to myself as I sat on the little rock.

Still, the image of Junho sitting and waiting in the studio lingered in my mind. How could I disappoint him? I would talk it over with Bokhi and Teacher Yun. Perhaps they would tell me what I should do. But I knew they would only gape in amazement at my lack of propriety. They would conclude that I had lost all respect for myself and for my family, and, in turn, they would lose respect for me. I couldn't let that happen. It was only Saturday, and I had six more days to think about it. Deciding to give myself some time, I hid the letter at the bottom of my school bag.

For the next few days, I tried desperately to decide what I should do. Bokhi said I seemed troubled and complained that I was too quiet. Teacher Yun and Mother also noticed how quiet I had grown and kept asking me if I felt all right. I assured them I was fine, but Friday came all too quickly, and I still did not know what to do. Torn, I decided just to see where my feet would take me when the time came.

When our last class ended, I sprang out the door without waiting for Bokhi and without saying goodbye to Teacher Yun.

"Sookan, Sookan," Bokhi called as she ran to catch up with me. "Please talk to me. We always used to be able to share our troubles with each other. Please talk to me. I know you have a problem. Tell me what it is! Remember I am two years older. I may know better. I can help you."

I couldn't respond.

"Are you mad at me? Don't you like me anymore?" she asked.

"Oh, Bokhi, I still like you as much as I always have. I don't have a problem. Can I just go now? Why don't you go home?"

"Are we drifting apart because I'm not Catholic and am not in the choir with you? Is that it?"

I knew Bokhi was just trying to provoke me into talking to her. She had guessed it had something to do with the choir. Though I tried to maintain composure, I couldn't help snapping impatiently, "Bokhi, I am fine! There is nothing I can tell you. I myself do not know. I'll see you tomorrow."

Bokhi saw the cold look in my eyes and she turned away. I instantly felt horrible, and stood watching her rush away. She didn't look back. I knew I had hurt her as never before. I thought of running after her, linking arms with her, and telling her all about Junho. But I just stood there and watched her disappear from sight. My callousness surprised me. I was ashamed at how eager I had been to be rid of her. For the first time, I had a secret that I couldn't share with my best friend. I wondered if I was turning into a bad person. I didn't know what I felt or thought anymore. But I kept walking, and quickly turned down the street to the photo studio.

The sign beckoned: "Beautiful Pictures, Every Time."

In a small glass case were pictures of proud grandparents surrounded by their large families, happy couples on their wedding day, and children celebrating their 100th day of life. I thought of passing right by as I had so many times before. But instead, I reached out and pushed open the wooden door. Inside the small hallway was a set of steep narrow stairs that seemed to shout down to me, "Turn back! Go see Bokhi!" But I climbed the stairs defiantly, and my trembling hand pushed open a frosted glass door on the second floor.

As the door swung open, I saw Junho sitting on a wooden bench in front of the studio's cameras. It was a different world in there with the sunny, filtered lights. "You're here!" Junho exclaimed, looking at once relieved and elated.

"I want a picture of us together," he said to the photographer as he motioned for me to hurry and sit next to him.

Grinning cheerfully, the photographer said, "Good! good! Perfect timing. Come sit right next to him. No, no, a bit closer, a little more. Closer. Good!" Then he came over to twist Junho's shoulders slightly so that his left shoulder was tucked behind my right shoulder. Rushing back to look through his camera lens, he said, "Beautiful! Now tilt your head a bit toward his. Oh, that's very sweet. Tilt your head toward hers, too. Just a bit. Ah, perfect!"

The shutter clicked. Smiling contentedly, the enthusiastic photographer congratulated himself. "What a picture! The composition, the angles, the light — it's a masterpiece. You will see. It will be ready in a few days."

Dazed from the bright lights and numb from the whole experience, I followed Junho down the narrow stairs in silence. When we reached the bottom, we stood for a minute, looking at each other. Junho seemed calm and happy, and I felt so close to him.

"I'm glad you came," he whispered. "I can't wait to see the picture." I nodded in silence, and he suddenly grew somber. "I am afraid we don't have too many days left together," he said with a heavy sigh. "Well, you must hurry to make the hike up the mountain before sundown." I couldn't say a thing. I felt so numb and confused. "You go first and take the short cut," he said. "I will go the long way." He didn't want to take any chances now. I smiled and quickly left.

That night, I ate a huge dinner, not because I was hungry but because I feared that if I looked up from my plate, Mother would know that I was keeping something from her. As I busily chewed my food, my heart throbbed. I had never disobeyed her, and had never kept a secret from her. That had all changed today. My shoulders ached as if I were carrying a ton of bricks. How long would I feel this way? Should I tell her about the photo studio? It would hurt her and worry her, and now, it was too late anyway. What had possessed me to do such a daring thing? And how could I be so dishonest? As I ate the last bite of my dinner, Junho's smiling face appeared before me. Was Junho worth all this pain? Yes, he certainly was, I concluded.

"You still don't look quite right, but your appetite has certainly come back stronger than ever," Mother said. She put her hand against my forehead and asked, "Is something troubling you? Anything you want to get off your chest?"

For the first time, I lied. "No, nothing at all. I'm fine, Mother," I said, giving her a big hug. I wondered if she would still love me as much if she knew that I had betrayed her for Junho.

Chapter Eight

The following Sunday, after Mass, Haerin asked Junho and me to put the hymnals in the closet as she had something important to attend to. While I collected the books, Junho drew near and whispered, "Stay around. Maybe we can talk here after everyone leaves. I have the picture." He patted his chest pocket gently.

Once everyone had left, we sat down across from each other at the back of the church, and he handed me a small white envelope. Trembling, I slowly pulled out the photo. The second I saw it, I was filled with delight. It was a beautiful picture of us, smiling, without a care in the world. A soft white glow around our faces made the picture look warm and natural. I had no idea I had looked this content and peaceful sitting next to Junho in the studio. Junho looked handsomer than ever and I couldn't think of a better souvenir of our friendship. I felt light-headed and I blushed as I stared at the picture. Although we had never even held hands, I felt infinitely close to him.

As I sat mesmerized, he whispered gently, "Isn't it a

wonderful picture of us? We look alike, don't you think? Now you will never forget me. Don't be afraid. I know I asked you to do something highly unusual, but it's all right. We stand side by side at choir, and here we're just sitting together side by side. There is nothing wrong with that."

I nodded my head in agreement, but I was unconvinced, and doubt started growing within me. We were not merely sitting together. This picture was sweeter than any wedding picture I had ever seen. I was terribly afraid of what others might say if they ever saw it.

Junho looked into my eyes and reassured me. "These pictures are only for us and no one else shall see them."

When we were just about to say goodbye and go our separate ways, a church lady saw us smiling and putting things into our pockets. Walking hurriedly toward us, she shouted, "What are you doing, whispering in an empty church all by yourselves? You should have left long ago. What are you hiding? Let me see." She stretched out her hand.

Junho walked quickly toward her, blocking me from sight. "Oh, please don't worry. It's me, Junho, the one who sings your favorite songs. We are on our way." She smiled at Junho, but she gave me the evil eye.

"What's going on?" said Haerin as she walked into the room and saw the lady's sour face. "Tell me what's going on!" The lady walked away, shaking her head.

Placing his hand on Haerin's shoulder, Junho chuckled and said, "Nothing for you to be concerned about, my little sister. You are back just in time. The hymnals are all arranged in the closet. Let's go home."

Haerin shot a puzzled glance in my direction, but she did as her older brother said, and led the way out the door. I wondered if she would try to talk to the church lady. I prayed she would never find out about the picture. She would be furious to find that we had kept a secret from her, and she would be horribly jealous of my special relationship with Junho. She would feel betrayed by Junho, but she would forgive him; she would blame it all on me. She was intrigued by my life experience and she needed me to sing in her choir, but she had no great affection for me. I think she knew Junho liked singing duets with me, but I don't think she suspected anything more. She would surely not allow anything to come between her and her *oppa* if she could help it. What would happen to my friendship with Junho if she ever managed to find the photo?

While I walked in fear and discomfort, Junho looked into my eyes and smiled, whistling a tune to harmonize with Haerin's humming. I took a deep breath, and tried to convince myself that Junho would never let Haerin find out about the picture.

With my secret safely tucked away, I resumed my after-school walks with Bokhi. Bokhi walked with me but didn't talk much for several days. I would catch her staring at me, wondering what it was that I had hidden from her that day. But after a while, she gave up as it was clear to her that I wouldn't talk about it. We began to study together and test each other on English and French vocabulary again. I was thankful that she didn't pry, though I felt guilty for having hurt her and for having kept this secret from her. But I just knew I couldn't talk of Junho. It would sound outrageous, and I could picture Bokhi gasping with surprise and disapproval. Besides, my relationship with Junho was so special; I was afraid that if I told anyone, something might happen, and our friendship would no longer be so precious.

The following Saturday, Inchun left the house early for his science field trip. He had been collecting rocks, fossils, rare plants, roots, and even caterpillars. Before I had even begun to get ready for choir practice, Mother said, "Sookan, now that Inchun has left, I need to talk with you. You are not going to be in the choir anymore. Sit down." Her face was drawn and her voice was flat.

I felt as if a huge boulder had been hurled at me, crushing all that I cherished in life. I knew it had something to do with the picture. My heart tightened and my face burned. I sat still, with my head hung low. I saw thousands of fingers pointing at me and I heard the mocking laughter of the mountain people as they said, "Look at her. She's the one. She has no scruples. She had a picture taken with a boy, and she hid it from her mother. What a bad daughter! What anguish she is causing her poor mother!"

"Sookan, do not look so frightened. I am not angry with you. But I am disappointed that you kept this from me. I know you are at the age where your heart rules. But, you could have told me, even after the photo was taken. Then, I would have been somewhat better prepared to deal with Mrs. Min's harsh words. Anyway, it doesn't matter now. It's all over. And I did tell Junho's parents how I felt."

At the mention of Junho's parents, I stared panic-stricken at Mother. She told me that yesterday afternoon, a letter was left on her desk at the refugee center. It was an invitation from Dr. and Mrs. Min, Junho's parents, to come for afternoon tea. Mother guessed that she was being summoned to explain my friendship with Junho. She did not know the Min family and there was no other reason for them to ask her to tea, she said. Mother knew that these unpleasant and awkward discussions sometimes occurred, but she decided not to make too much of it. After all, we were both just high-school students and our friendship was very innocent, she thought. There was certainly no reason for alarm. So Mother went, prepared to defend our friendship.

Dr. Min greeted Mother cordially, and had her take a seat. Mrs. Min then stormed into the room, threw the photo in front of Mother, and shouted, "Look at this! Just look at this horrible sight! Our good son is ruined! Your daughter is bad news. Look what she did. She lured my boy to the studio and coaxed him into sitting with her like lovebirds. We have been raising him to become a respected doctor just like his father and his grandfather. Now all he talks about is becoming a priest. He has gone crazy. This picture explains it all."

In shock and disbelief, Mother picked up the photo. She stared at it, bewildered that I could have behaved so rashly. She was ready to apologize to the Mins and rush home to scold me, but she was struck by how lovely the photo was. She couldn't put it down.

Instead, she spoke to Dr. Min, who sat in pensive silence. "Dr. Min, I hope you are not angry about this photo. Please do not punish your son for this. To me, it looks like nothing more than an innocent photo taken to preserve their brief friendship during this turbulent time. The war has brought us together, but soon we will all be going in different directions. I believe their friendship is pure. They must find comfort in each other during these uncertain and sad times. They need friends to talk to of their dreams, fears, and sorrows. As for your son, he is a fine, intelligent, young man, and I am sure he knows his mind and knows what he wants out of life. My little girl cannot make up his mind for him. She knows only what she wants to do."

Dr. Min's face softened and he glanced at his angry wife. Looking a bit embarrassed, he said, "Thank you for coming," and he sighed. "I will give this photo back to my son. You are only young once." He reached to take the photo back from Mother, but Mrs. Min snatched it away.

"Not if I can help it!" she shrieked. "He will not have it!"

Dr. Min graciously escorted Mother to the street, apologizing for his wife's behavior and thanking Mother again.

Filled with shame for putting my mother through such a humiliating experience, I took the photo out from its hiding place and gave it to her. She patted my head and unfolded the many layers of wrapping. She looked at it again for a long time and smiled calmly. "How peaceful and happy you both look. I'm sure even Mrs. Min's bitter heart would melt if she looked at this picture long enough. You can keep it, but make sure no one else sees it."

With a deep breath, she said, "It's not the end of the world. It *is* all over now. But you must remember that most people do not understand a special friendship between a boy and a girl of your age. You must behave like a proper young lady now." Then she shook her head with a smile of resignation. "My daughter, I must say, you are a daring child. You always were. I never know quite what you will do next; you're a constant source of wonder to me. But, for now, your old mother has had quite enough excitement."

She threw her arms open and hugged me. "Promise me you will not do such a thing again. If you do, at least don't keep it a secret from me." She looked me in the eye sternly, and I nodded, intending to keep *this* promise to her at all costs.

From that day on, I did not go to choir practice or to any of the choir Masses. Every Sunday I went to Mass at dawn with Mother to avoid running into any choir members. Each time Mother and I walked back home, I wanted to ask if she thought Junho would really become a priest. But since my friendship with Junho had caused her so much trouble already, I decided it would be best to keep silent. Perhaps he had just said that to annoy his mother. Or had he decided to become a priest once he heard that I planned to be a nun? He had never mentioned it to me, but I remembered how interested he was in philosophy. Did he ever have that discussion about Thomas Aquinas with Father Lee? Had Father Lee influenced his decision? Junho often spoke with admiration of Father Lee's dedication to the people. My brother Hanchun, who had spent lots of time with Father Lee before the war, had also decided he wanted to be a priest.

One Sunday morning when I was returning from dawn Mass with mother, I saw Haerin rushing toward the church with an armful of hymnals. Her large, pink hair ribbon was flying in the wind, her long skirt ballooned as she ran, and her baton case swung at her side. I could almost hear Junho's sweet voice. I missed our singing and talking.

When Haerin saw me watching her, she glared at me disdainfully. She tossed her shiny head of black hair, and sneered at me as if I had sullied something that belonged to her. The look in her eyes stayed in my mind as I climbed up the mountain. I realized it was she who either spoke to the church lady or found the photo and told her mother. It was probably she who placed the invitation to tea on my mother's desk. She would see to it that no one stood between her and her *oppa*.

Chapter Nine

Our teachers scheduled many evening classes and often taught right through the weekend to help us make up for all the time we had lost because of the war. They were determined to bring their lesson plans in line with those of the Pusan schoolteachers. Delighted, I eagerly attended all the extra classes unless Mother complained that I would be home too late to climb the mountain. During the little free time I had, I helped Mother cultivate our little garden. She was an expert on plants and created a garden that was always in bloom. As the roses wilted, the lilies began to open.

Then, in July 1953, the armistice agreement was signed and everything seemed to revert to the way it had been before the war broke out. The area north of the 38th Parallel was to be again under Communist rule and the southern portion under democratic rule. Korea would remain divided, but at least there would be peace. As soon as the news was out, the tens of thousands of refugees frantically prepared to return to their homes, anxious to find their missing relatives and to rebuild their lives.

Everything was chaos once again. Everyone was in a frenzy to pack and leave. I wanted to see Bokhi and Teacher Yun, and perhaps arrange to take the same train back up to Seoul. But when I told Mother that I was going to look for them, she said, "Sookan, they've probably already left. The refugees by the seashore got news of the armistice first, and immediately packed and left. There are so many stories of orphans crying in the streets of Seoul with no one to take care of them, not to mention all the dead and wounded. I'm sure Teacher Yun is worried about her nieces and nephews, and went back as fast as she could. These are difficult times, and we don't have the luxury of saying goodbye. We will find Teacher Yun and Bokhi back in Seoul."

Would my life ever be orderly enough to afford me the chance for a simple goodbye? After listening to Mother, I felt silly for daring to dream of traveling on the same train with Bokhi and Teacher Yun.

The narrow mountain path was filled with refugees carrying their meager belongings. Many people were camped out at the station in order to assure themselves a place on the 4:00 A.M. train, the only train of the day. While witnessing the frenetic exodus, Mother, Inchun, and I began packing our few belongings. Inchun wrapped some of the special rocks he had collected on his science expeditions, and I carefully tucked away my book *Half Moon*, the photo, and some of the shells that Bokhi and I had managed to collect at the seashore. Mother took several little bags of seeds.

"I have been collecting these seeds ever since I arrived in Pusan. Some of these flowers are very different from what we have in Seoul." She even had a bag of sunflower seeds. She said the sunflowers in Pusan were yellower and larger.

Cloaked in darkness, our empty little hut looked sad and lonely. Mother closed the door carefully and gave it a gentle pat, whispering softly, "Well, goodbye. It's time for us to go." For the last time, the three of us stood there staring at the humble shack that safely housed us for two and a half years. I had grown attached to our little home, and I looked at it with deep affection. What would happen to all these empty huts? Would the Pusan residents tear them down to use for firewood? Or would the wind and snow and rain slowly eat away at them? Maybe the morning glories, sunflowers, and cosmos would grow wild, a lasting gift from the refugees to this once barren mountain. Yes, I decided, all these flowers would forever decorate the mountain, luring even the animals back.

I looked at the dark mountain across the way to the spot where the shouting poet used to stand. I said goodbye to him in my heart. It felt very strange leaving Pusan. Suddenly, everything that had happened in the last two and a half years here felt like a dream. We, along with all the other refugees, were now in a great hurry to go back to Seoul, where we would have to start all over again. I thought of Bokhi and her sand castles. She was right in a sense. We had built our school, our homes, and our lives here, and now we just had to leave them all behind, to be washed away by time. I wondered what would happen to the Ewha School we had built by the seashore. This life of constant change and uncertainty filled me with frustration. But then, I remembered the cheery, resounding voice of my shouting poet. He wouldn't like me to leave the mountain with such sadness and bitterness. To please him, I quickly imagined a lush, green mountain resounding with the echoes of the White Giraffe.

"Come on, no time to linger about," Mother said. "Let's hurry and hope we can get on this train."

In the dark, with only the light of the pale moon, we slipped and slid down the dirt path for the last time. I looked over at the well, which seemed bare without the long queue of women and children. When we arrived at the bottom of the hill, I glanced over to the far right where Junho's brick house stood. It was dark and quiet, indifferent to my departure. I lingered for a second, wishing that Browny might start to bark and that Junho might peer out the window and see me leaving. Mother pulled my arm, and we rushed to the train station.

As we expected, the station was swarming with people, shouting and pushing. The long train had already arrived and was hissing loudly. The agitated conductor impatiently blew his shrill whistle, making me wince in pain. Luckily we were pushed along by the crowds toward a door of the train. We hurriedly jumped on, and even managed to get seats all together by a window.

It started to drizzle, casting a gray haze over Pusan. I

stuck my head out the window to feel the gentle mist, and I looked out at the city of Pusan one last time. Would I ever see this place again? Would I ever see Junho again? What would we find when we got back to Seoul? I wondered if Father and my brothers would be there waiting for us. I wondered if there would be anything left of our house. Once again, I was headed for the unknown.

My hair was getting wet, and I wondered why I kept hanging out the window. Did I expect Junho to appear? I hadn't seen him for months, not even once since my mother's visit with his parents. There was no way he would know that I was leaving today. So many refugees had already left in the past few days, and many more would be leaving in the weeks to follow.

Mother tugged at my skirt. "Sookan, sit down and close the window. The rain is coming in, and besides, it's not safe." I realized then that almost half my body was hanging out the window. But as I carefully pulled my shoulders back through the window, I saw in the distance, buried in the crowds, a young man in a tan raincoat, holding flowers over his head to keep them from being crushed. I leaned all the way out the window again. He was squinting in the rain, looking left and right in desperation. It was Junho!

"Junho, Junho, over here!" I shouted, waving my arms back and forth. "Here I am! Over here!"

He finally saw me and his face brightened. He pushed

through the crowds and ran up to me. Holding the flowers up as high as he could, he said, "Here, take it, Sookan! It's for you. I've been coming here for the last couple of days, hoping to find you. I'm sorry for everything. I still have the picture here." He tapped his chest pocket and added, "Read the poem. It's inside."

The train whistled loudly, and a puff of thick white smoke rose into the air. The conductor shouted at Junho to stand clear of the platform. The train jerked forward, preparing to pull away. "I have our picture, too, here in my bag," I yelled, and I lifted my bag to show him. He smiled, nodding his head.

"Take care of yourself!" he shouted, his voice quivering and his handsome face turning somber. He waved and I could see his mouth moving, but I could no longer hear what he was saying. The train let out a long, loud whistle and began picking up speed. I watched Junho desperately trying to run alongside the train. He started to push through the crowds, waving his arms wildly, but he quickly faded into the distance.

"Sit down," Mother said, as she brusquely pulled me in and shut the window with a bang. Then, a second later, she said more calmly, "It's not safe to hang out the window like that and I cannot afford to lose you. Open your flowers. They smell so sweet."

I gently tore open the paper, and saw a single, crushed white lily with an envelope tied to the stem. I quickly put the envelope in my skirt pocket as I wanted to read it later when Mother and Inchun dozed off. The sweet perfume of the lily soothed my racing heart. I caressed the velvety petals that had gotten crushed and smeared with yellow pollen. The trees, houses, and hills that passed before me seemed like nothing more than a blurry line through my tear-filled eyes. I wished that I had some magical power to make the train go back to the station, where I would find Junho standing with his head hung low. I would ask him to hop on the train for a trip to Seoul. What a fine trip that would be!

Leaning their heads back, Mother and Inchun closed their eyes. Carefully, I took the white envelope from my skirt pocket. In his fine handwriting, Junho had written:

My White Lily

Amidst the barren fields,
Dark and gray with endless gloom,
Stood alone, a white lily in bloom,
Fragile but resilient,
Swaying in the wind,
Exuding its sweet scent.
Pure and simple
You are my white lily,
My hope, my strength.

Your everlasting friend,
Junho. Summer 1953

I read it over and over. He had signed it "Your ever-lasting friend," and I clung to those words. I wondered if

I would ever see him again. Drawing the sweet perfume of the white lily deep into my lungs, I thought of the choir picnic when Haerin asked him to pick the yellow lilies.

Overwhelmed with memories, I looked out the window and watched the rice paddies and small farmhouses draw closer only to fade quickly into the distance. The sun was shining through the rain-streaked window. How strange life was! Everything that had happened during the last two and a half years had seemed like a distant dream, but with this letter, it all suddenly welled up before me: the shouting poet, Junho, the long climbs up and down the mountain, the Ewha School by the seashore. The lily and the poem made it all real for me; now I knew my memories would stay with me forever. I held the lily and the poem to my heart, and concluded that my life was not a series of sand castles. There was meaning to life, and precious memories even amidst the sadness.

A bright spot of sunlight leaped from Mother's clasped hands to Inchun's dark hair. How kind of them to give me these moments of peace with no questions asked. Mother was now pensively looking out the window with her eyebrows tightly knit and her upper teeth gnawing on her lower lip. I could tell how worried and frightened she was. Inchun stared at me as I studied Mother's expression. He began to whistle, then stopped and smiled. I knew he had come up with an idea to distract Mother.

"*Nuna,* what are you going to do with that disgusting,

97

wilted flower? Do you want me to take care of it?" Then he motioned to the window with his chin.

I gave him an angry stare, placed the flower on Mother's lap, and pleaded for help. She put her hands over the lily and said with a sudden smile, "Oh, you two are keeping me going. Maybe we *will* find the rest of the family in Seoul."

Relieved to see Mother smile and talk, Inchun kept taunting me. "*Nuna*, can I see that mushy stuff you read for hours? Junho probably copied something from a dead French poet and you think he's talking about you. Can I see it?" Mother ruffled Inchun's hair and he grinned.

The Seoul train station was up ahead and the platform was jammed with people hoping to find their loved ones on the train. Their anxious faces searched every window. As the train came to a stop, we gathered our belongings and battled the crowds. We were pushed off the train and propelled through the streets of Seoul. No one called after us.

Everything around the station had been bombed, and nothing looked familiar. Bricks, wood, and cement blocks were stacked everywhere. The city looked like one giant construction site. We headed down what we thought was the road to our house. Trucks carrying lumber wove through the streets and honked loudly at us. Many small tents and temporary dwellings had been set up to shelter small children and old folks. Women and children were cooking in front of some of these meager homes, watchful of trucks and passers-by that might disturb their preparations.

After a long walk, we made it through the busy streets and turned down the familiar little dead-end road that led to our house at the foot of Namsan Mountain. I looked up and saw a part of our gray tiled roof from behind our big cherry tree. What a relief to see our house still standing! We walked as fast as we could, but the street was covered with broken bricks, fallen branches, chunks of concrete, and broken glass.

Memories of running from the house during the last bombing came rushing back. Mother had kept screaming for me to hurry. The sounds of sirens, airplanes, and exploding bombs had rung in my head, and whenever I looked back, I could see buildings collapsing behind me. I shuddered as I remembered the awful smell of smoke. To rid myself of these memories, I gazed up at the clear blue sky. How thankful I was for the peaceful sky above me.

Chapter Ten

We finally reached the big stone steps leading up to our house. The thick, cherry-wood doors, scorched and marred by gaping holes, still hung stubbornly from their hinges and retained some of their former elegance. The brass door knockers shaped like dragons were blackened and hung askew, but tenaciously claimed their place. Overwhelmed with relief and excitement, I ran up the stairs, all twelve of them, and stepped over the broken branches and pieces of stone strewn about on the steps.

"Sookan, no!" Mother shouted as I was about to open the door. "Wait. It could cave in. Wait."

Suddenly a thin man appeared in one of the side windows. "Finally! You're back!" a voice exclaimed. It was Jaechun! "Mother, don't worry, we already secured the doors," he shouted. I could hear him running to let us in.

It was like a dream come true. Inchun and Mother rushed up, and Hanchun, Hyunchun, and Jaechun came running to greet us. I stared at them in awe. They looked so different from the last time I had seen them. They were so much older, taller, and thinner, and their skin was dark and leathery. Their T-shirts were covered with sawdust and ash, and they all had pencils stuck behind their ears, and tools in hand.

Mother's mouth hung open as she stared wide-eyed at her three older sons. "Can this be possible?" she gasped. "All three of you safe and sound and waiting for us here at the house!"

All I could do was stand and watch as she hugged all three of them and cried with joy. Jaechun lifted Inchun way up in the air and spun him around. Hanchun patted me on the head and pinched my cheeks as if I were still a little girl. "Oh, how big you got!" he said.

"And your father?" Mother asked, expecting him to appear any minute.

"We thought he was with you," Hanchun blurted out.

Dead silence fell over us all. Hyunchun cleared his throat and said, "It's still too early. It'll take a while for everyone to make it back home."

Mother's face grew somber. She looked down at her hands and didn't seem to have heard a word he said. "We must check all the hospitals. He must be sick somewhere. That's the only thing that would keep him from us," she said emphatically.

"Mother, there you go worrying again," Jaechun said. "I bet you thought *we* were all lost, but here we are safe and sound. Father will come. Let's wait a few days."

Mother smiled sheepishly at her sons.

"The three of us just met up here at the house over the past four days," Hanchun said. He told us that when we had all run from the house, he, Hyunchun, and Jaechun had been following right behind us. But all too quickly, they had lost sight of us. Retreating army trucks were jamming the streets, and several officers were calling for men to join the army and help fight the enemy. Each of them had ended up jumping on a separate truck, and from that moment on, had been separated. Hanchun and Hyunchun spent most of their time near the battle fields. Jaechun, because of his poor health, worked as a translator for a war correspondent near the battle zone.

Hanchun went on to say that over the past few days, they had been busy clearing the road, the steps, and the yard. When they first arrived, they could barely make their way up to the house. Now they had begun repairing the inside of the house.

Hanchun carefully opened the front door. We stepped inside, and found ourselves standing in a large, empty space. All of the walls had crumbled, and there were mounds of debris gathered in the corners. In the piles of rubble, I saw pieces of our furniture, broken records, and clothes; everything was an ashen gray and was barely identifiable. The wide glass doors that led out to Mother's garden had shattered, and the metal door frames were rusted and twisted like an odd sculpture. One whole corner of the house was missing, and I could see straight out to the backyard. Mother's pretty greenhouse in the far corner of the garden was now just a pile of broken glass. The grapevine trellis, under which I had loved to read while eating the deep purple grapes, was now a heap of charred wood. The front doors had been terribly deceiving. After seeing all this destruction, I was amazed that the doors still stood.

"It's going to take a long time," Hanchun said, "but we can make this place livable again. For now, we should all sleep in the basement."

For the next few weeks, while we were hard at work repairing our house, my brothers secretly took turns checking all the hospitals and information centers for any news of Father. They didn't say anything to Mother, and she never asked. She just kept hoping for good news.

Father Lee finally discovered the sad truth. Father's name was on a list of men who had died during the bombing. Mother did not cry when she heard the news. She somberly stared down at her hands, just as she had when we first returned to the house and learned that Father was not there. I think she knew then.

I ran out and stood staring at the duck pond that Father had made for Mother. Out of smooth, gray pebbles, he had built it in the shape of the Korean peninsula. It had been a surprise for her birthday. I furiously began cleaning the pond, and Mother eventually came out and joined me. Thinking of Father, we worked in silence for several days to restore the little pond. Jaechun brought three ducklings home one day, and Mother often sat by the pond and fed them. Whenever she got up, the ducks would waddle after her into the garden.

Jaechun repaired my corner room, which once had large picture windows on two sides so that I could see the city of Seoul. Knowing how much I loved looking out at the sky, he managed to obtain several large plates of glass, which he pieced together. It was far from what it used to be, but I once again had a full view of the sky and of downtown Seoul. In the basement I found a small broken desk, a brass candleholder, and a rickety chair that Jaechun had nailed back together. I took out *Half Moon*, which held the dried petals of my white lily, and I placed it on the desk. I had safely tucked Junho's picture away in my bookbag to keep it from my protective older brothers.

Fortunately, the Ewha School had not been damaged much, and it soon reopened. I was happy to see so many friends I hadn't seen in three years, and we shouted and embraced. We didn't speak of those who weren't present, for none of us wanted to hear more bad news. I was glad to see Bokhi there, as I hadn't seen her since we left Pusan. She was still living with her old aunt and uncle, and now many of her first and second cousins had come to live with them too. Her aunt and uncle were pleased to take care of them, and, in return, the young people worked hard to repair what was left of their house.

Teacher Yun worked harder than ever to get Ewha back up and running. As the oldest survivor in her family, she now had many little nieces and nephews to take care of at home. She often had to bring the little ones to school, and Bokhi and I babysat during recess.

Mother spent several days sorting through the piles of rubble in our house. I occasionally joined her, but it was a constant reminder of the precious things we used to have, none of which seemed salvageable. I threw everything back in distaste and wondered why Mother kept at it so diligently. I wanted to ask, but she looked so sad that I felt she just needed something to do to get over her grief. After she had gone through the piles in the house, she started carefully digging up every inch of the backyard, like an archeologist.

I joined her for a while, and I did recover one thing I couldn't part with. It was my Luxy's wooden bowl. Three-quarters of it, that is. It was broken and dirty, but I took it to my room anyway. Luxy used to bring this wooden bowl to me on hot days and whimper for cool water. I missed her.

When Jaechun saw the remains of Luxy's bowl, clean and shiny, on my desk, he said gently, "Sookan, you do know Luxy is alive and well, don't you?"

"No, why didn't you tell me sooner?" I said as tears started streaming down my face. "I've been wondering all this time, but was afraid to ask. How do you know? I have been afraid to help Mother dig up the backyard. I thought I might find Luxy buried there."

Jaechun told me that as he was running out of the house that day, he heard Luxy whimpering. He grabbed her and rushed out into the crowds. An army officer stuck his head out of a Jeep and shouted, "Handsome boxer you have there. Is he well trained?"

"Yes, sir! She's very intelligent and obeys orders."

The officer looked at Luxy's clear brown eyes and

cocked ears and said, "Hop on. You can't run with the dog like that." They rode all the way to the army base. Jaechun was immediately assigned some work translating, and the officer decided to keep Luxy. Jaechun said he often saw Luxy riding around in the Jeep with the officer, and she seemed proud and happy. Every time she passed Jaechun, she barked to say hello. After about a month, the officer was transferred to a safer zone, and took Luxy with him. Jaechun was sure that Luxy was still alive and that she was being well cared for by the officer.

I wasn't sure how much of his story to believe, but it was comforting. I hoped he was right and that Luxy was safe and happy somewhere.

Mother went on digging up the backyard for days. She examined every rag and every piece of wood, pottery, or metal she found. Occasionally I saw her smile as she put something in her pocket. I still didn't know what she was doing.

Finally, she proudly held out her treasures for me to see. She had found a piece of her gold bracelet, twisted and flattened. Her gold butterfly pin was mostly intact, except for the wings, which were broken. She even found her silver hair pin, crushed flat and caked with dirt.

"I have finally been rewarded for all that digging. I found these in the most unlikely places. They were buried deep in the earth. The bomb's force was tremendous."

"They're all broken and dirty. What good are they?" I said with disappointment.

"Mr. Han, the jewelry craftsman, can melt these pieces down and make something new. He will buy these from me."

Mother was right. The jeweler did buy those scraps from her, and she earned enough money for a special Requiem Mass for my father. She asked Father Lee to have the organist and the choir there. She ordered a large bundle of fresh flowers and arranged for refreshments afterwards for all the relatives and friends who came to the Mass.

Myungdong Cathedral was filled with people. All the women sat on the left side and the men on the right. I looked over at my four brothers, who all looked very handsome. Mother and I stood across from them. Just this once, I wished we could all sit together. I felt terribly sad and wanted the whole family together. But that was not allowed.

Teacher Yun, who was Presbyterian, and Bokhi, who was Buddhist, cautiously walked into the cathedral and sat together at the end of a pew. They bowed to Mother when we looked over. I could tell Bokhi was scared to be in a Catholic church for the first time. Behind Inchun was his science teacher, with whom he had spent so much time in Pusan. He gently touched Inchun on the shoulder to say hello, and Inchun turned and bowed.

Standing next to his three older brothers, Inchun looked very grown up. He was now one of the men. He did everything with our older brothers these days. He played basketball with them and went hiking with them.

On Sundays, he went to Mass with them. They were inseparable. It was as if they had made a pact to spend every possible minute together to make up for the time they had been apart during the war. Inchun loved being with his older brothers and no longer had any reason to spend time with me. Though he still loved me, I was a girl, after all, and he had little business hanging around with me. I saw Mother look over at the boys, and suddenly I felt lonesome, alone, and different from all of them.

Under the morning light, the tall stained-glass windows of Myungdong Cathedral cast bright blue and purple shadows on our faces. The organ started to play as Father Lee slowly walked down the aisle in his black funeral vestment. How sad that our first big Mass together since we had returned from Pusan had to be for such a somber occasion. I faithfully mouthed the prayers and songs and walked up to the altar for communion, but my mind was a million miles away. I felt anxious and confused. I was tired of this war that kept haunting me. I looked at the beautiful cathedral and remembered how delighted I used to be to come here. The wondrous stained-glass windows depicting the saints used to fill me with awe. The sun filtering through these colored windows and the resounding organ music used to transport me to another world. But, now, I just felt unhappy and restless.

I heard Father Lee say, "He has moved to the next world, for God has called him. But his spirit is still with us. His spirit will always be with those he loves. So let us rejoice in his joining God in Heaven."

Suddenly, I felt distanced from everything that was going on around me, and I just wanted to go far away. I knew I had to do something, and as I stood there, I decided I must push forward with my plans to go abroad, to see new and wonderful things.

Life in Seoul slowly returned to normal. Hanchun went back to veterinary school at Seoul University part-time, and worked part-time as a doctor's assistant. Jaechun took literature classes at the nearby university in the mornings, and in the afternoons he worked at the CIA office as a translator. He grew very serious, and never breathed a word about his work. He would come home late at night and lock himself up in his room with mysterious documents. Whenever we went into his room to see him, everything was carefully hidden away. Hyunchun started attending the foreign language school two days a week, and the rest of the time he taught at a local typing school. Between the three of them, they brought home enough money for us to live on.

Still determined to go to the United States for college, I kept studying as hard as I could. After Mass one day, I waited by the side door of Father Lee's vestibule. When he emerged, I asked him if he would speak to Bishop Roh on my behalf to help me obtain a scholarship to one of the Catholic colleges in the United States.

"Your mother told me you wanted to study abroad, Sookan. But you will have to pass the government tests first, and they are so difficult that many college graduates I know are taking the test for the second or third time. Why are you in such a hurry? You are still too young. Go to Ewha University for the next four years and then we will talk about it."

He must have noticed how hurt and disappointed I was, because he then said he would discuss it with my brothers and my mother later in the week. He was sure, though, that they would agree I was too young to leave home.

I enrolled myself in English classes that were given in the evenings downtown. After finishing the day at Ewha, I would head straight to my English grammar, conversation, and composition classes and not get home until late at night. Mother always kept dinner warm for me. As I ate, she would fill me in on all the news at home and in the neighborhood.

She often asked me if I could stop attending my evening classes so I could come home earlier and spend some time with the family. But I refused to give in, and after a while, Mother stopped asking. Instead, she bought me a bunch of candles for my room so that I could study as late as I wished. The bombs had downed all the electrical lines, and it would take a while before we got power back because we were far away from the center of the city.

My intensive preparation for the government exam left me no time to spend with Bokhi after school. We always made sure to take walks together during recess, and hand in hand, we wandered the well-manicured gardens of Ewha. Bokhi no longer spoke of sand castles and pebbles. She was now too busy taking care of her new, large family. As the oldest girl in the family, she took care of her uncle and aunt and did all the housekeeping and cooking for her little cousins. Although she was busy with all of these responsibilities, she looked content and pretty. She often asked how my brothers were doing, and lately she seemed to show particular interest in Hyunchun. I had seen her looking over at him during the Requiem Mass, but I hadn't thought much about it. Now I started to notice how flushed she became whenever she asked about him.

Perhaps she felt the same way about Hyunchun as I had about Junho. I suddenly remembered Haerin and smiled. I would not be as jealous and protective as Haerin had been. I thought about it for a while, then said, "Bokhi, I've been having trouble in home economics class. I'm so behind on our final project that I haven't even finished embroidering the edges of the tablecloth yet. I like embroidery, but it takes so long and I just don't have the time lately."

"But you embroider so nicely," Bokhi said, trying to encourage me. "Mrs. Ho even said so when she gave you your interim grade. Before the war, you and I were the best in the whole school, remember?"

I looked around to make sure none of my classmates were around and said, "Don't tell Mrs. Ho, but my mother saw that I had fallen asleep over my embroidery, and she must have stayed up all night finishing my midterm project for me. When I woke up, it was ironed and folded and all packed. I just can't do it anymore." I sighed for effect.

When I got home that night, I told Mother that I was sure Bokhi was hopelessly in love with Hyunchun. Mother smiled and said, "Poor Bokhi! Hyunchun thinks of her as a little girl. He sees her as his kid sister's friend."

But I knew things would soon change. Bokhi now had an excuse to visit frequently. She immediately started coming over to help me with my embroidery. She came often in her pretty dresses. As the deadline for my project drew nearer, she started staying later and later. As she worked on my tablecloth, she chatted and laughed with my mother. I was glad to see Bokhi and my mother so happy in each other's company. Bokhi had lost her mother and my mother would soon be losing me, in a sense. It was not long before Hyunchun noticed how pretty and talented Bokhi was. Hyunchun had a sharp eye when it came to girls.

I realized that Bokhi no longer came to see me. As long as Hyunchun was home, I don't think she even noticed whether I was there or not. It was hard to be shoved aside, even though I was the one who had brought the situation about. Studying in my room, I could hear my mother, Bokhi, and Hyunchun talking. Hyunchun had started coming home earlier and earlier, and would check in on their progress. He had suddenly developed quite an interest in embroidery, and always seemed to have lots of questions. His hearty laughter blended with that of my mother and Bokhi, and I suddenly felt strange. I wanted to close my books and rush to join them. Better yet, I would take Bokhi out for a walk and come back alone to sit with Mother and Hyunchun myself.

A gust of cold wind blew through my open window, and the fresh air helped clear my head. I had to laugh. How silly I was being! Petty and jealous, just like someone I once knew! I smiled at the thought of Haerin yanking Junho's sleeve when Junho and I tried to linger and talk. I should be happy that my best friend, my brother, and my mother were getting along so well.

The irony of it all! I studied furiously so that I could leave here, while Bokhi tried so hard to become part of my family. I wondered why I wasn't happy staying at home and why I wanted so desperately to go far away.

Chapter Eleven

My three brothers worked continually on the house. They put walls back up so that each of us would have our own bedroom, as we had before. Hanchun began filling his room with medical textbooks, which delighted Inchun, who constantly borrowed them. With his colored pencils, Inchun would copy the diagrams of skeletons, labeling each bone with its Latin name. Jaechun once again started to collect all sorts of literature, as he used to before the war. He built himself a wall of bookshelves, which he quickly filled. Books in English, Russian, Chinese, Korean, and Japanese were neatly arranged in alphabetical order, just like a library. I checked Jaechun's book collection every day, and almost always found that something new had been added. He even picked up half-torn or charred books and placed them carefully on his shelves. He also began to collect classical music records, which he listened to as he read late into the night. I liked hearing the soft strains of Bach fill the house as I studied.

Hyunchun's room was bare. Until recently, he had not spent much time at home. His job teaching typing seemed to keep him busier and busier. Mother and I chuckled about his tremendous success at the typing school. We were sure that many girls registered for his class because of his good looks and charm rather than his teaching expertise. He typed no better than I did, and often looked at a book called *All You Need to Know About Typing*.

Every Sunday, we had a large family dinner and invited many friends and neighbors. Father Lee was a regular guest, and Teacher Yun and Bokhi often joined us. The dinners lasted for several hours, as the men all discussed their jobs, school, and, of course, international politics. Mother rushed back and forth from the kitchen, constantly bringing more hot food, tea, and warm rice wine. She beamed as she watched everyone enjoy her cooking, and she listened attentively to the discussions.

One Sunday evening, I left the table early to go study for the government test. The setting sun shone warmly on the wide pine boards in the hallway leading to my room. It seemed an inviting place to sit and relax, and so I sat down, basking in the setting sun and staring out the window at Mother's green garden. The sound of distant voices, laughter, and the rattling of chopsticks and dishes was comforting.

Why couldn't I just sit in the dining room with the rest of the family and enjoy being with them? Why was I always running around trying to learn more and do something different? Why did I want to leave and go so far away, especially now that everything seemed to be settling down? I always felt so empty, restless, and incomplete. What was I searching for? I didn't know exactly, but I felt I had to go away to find something that would fill the emptiness inside me.

I heard a knock on the front door. Jaechun answered the door, and then, I heard the murmur of men's voices. I remained in the hallway, and saw Jaechun walk back to the dining room. Mother then rushed to the door. "Oh, come in!" she said with surprise. "Oh, of course, this way." Mother and the guest stepped out of the front alcove into the hallway, which was within my view. The guest was Junho.

"Sookan," she called. "Look who's here! It's Junho. He wants to visit with you for a while." She led him to me. "You can either sit in the living room, or you can go to your room and talk. Your room is pretty at this hour with the sun setting."

She left Junho and went back to the dining room. Everyone in the dining room fell silent, and then I heard Mother's voice. I was sure Jaechun and my other brothers were demanding an explanation.

I was stunned to see Junho standing nervously in front of me. But my initial shock quickly turned to elation. How brave of him to come here and ask to see me. It was clever that he asked to see my mother first instead of asking for me. I wouldn't have known what to do.

"My room is around the corner, at the end of the hallway. It's small, but we can see the whole city from

116

there," I said nervously. He followed me, having already regained his composure.

Mother appeared right behind us, carrying a small chair to my room. She saw to it that we sat opposite each other at the table in my room, and said, "I'll bring you some tea. Junho, have you eaten? I can bring in some snacks."

"Oh, thank you, but I can only stay a few minutes," he said emphatically. "There is no need for you to bring any tea. I must be going very soon."

"Well, all right, then. But if you change your mind, it's no problem. I hope you will stay awhile." She walked out and closed the door halfway.

I remembered telling Junho that I lived at the foot of Namsan Mountain, but I had never expected him to show up here. Still amazed to see him before me, I stared at him, studying every noticeable change. His strong but gentle features were now more chiseled and distinct. There was a maturity and strength that I hadn't noticed before. He wore a dark suit, and clutched a Dongkuk University hat in his hand, so I knew he was a student there. From my room, I could even see some of his university's buildings.

"Would you like to put your hat down?"

He responded with an embarrassed smile. Though he seemed calm and composed, I saw his hand tremble as he placed his cap on the desk.

"How long have you been a student at Dongkuk

University? And how long have you been in Seoul?" I asked.

"I have been here several months. Since I graduated from Pusan High School. I live at a boarding house near the university."

"Oh," I said awkwardly. There were so many things I wanted to tell him. I wished I could tell him how happy and excited I was to see him. I wanted him to know how I treasured our photograph, and that I could recite his poem by heart. But I just sat quietly and watched the sunset from my window.

"You have a beautiful view from here. Your house must have been wonderful before the bombing," Junho said as he gazed at the orange sunset.

I smiled, and I felt like crying out, "Junho, how glad I am to see you! How often I thought about you!" But I couldn't seem to say a word. I was so frustrated at not being able to express my feelings.

"Are you planning to go abroad to study?" he asked with great urgency.

"Yes, I will leave as soon as I pass the government exam. I'm taking the test right after graduation. Father Lee promised to help me apply for a scholarship. I have filled out all the paperwork, and Teacher Yun has written my recommendation."

Then, anxious to know whether it was true that he wanted to be a priest, I asked, "What are you studying now? Medicine? Philosophy? Theology?"

Junho took a long breath and smiled. "Well, there

have been a lot of changes in my life since our last long conversation. I am not going to be a doctor. I am now studying literature at the university, but eventually I want to enter the seminary in Seoul."

I thought of how Dr. and Mrs. Min and Haerin must blame me. I knew they must miss him now that he was so far from Pusan. Was I responsible for his coming to Seoul? Had he decided to go to the seminary because I had told him of my plans to enter the convent? I thought of our days in Pusan together. He was always reading poetry, philosophy, and theology, and pondering the meaning of life. Perhaps he was meant to go to the seminary. I couldn't have changed all his plans.

Junho looked into my eyes and asked, "Do you still have the picture?"

"Yes!" I said.

"The poem, too?"

"Yes!"

"May I have them back? That is why I have come," he said in a low voice as he looked down at his hands.

"No, I can't give them to you. I won't!" I retorted, surprised and confused. My face grew hot. Why did he want them back?

Junho watched my face flush with anger and embarrassment. Then his eyes twinkled gently, and a smile came to his lips. He let out a long breath of relief.

"I must go now," he said, as he stood up.

Still sitting, I looked up at him and realized that he had not come for his poem or our picture at all. He just wanted to know if I still cared. He seemed relieved and happy that I wouldn't give them back to him. Sorry that I had ever doubted his everlasting friendship, I watched the last glorious rays of sun cling to the distant hills of Seoul. Although he didn't say that this was the last time we would see each other, I somehow sensed a finality in this meeting. I felt that he had come here to close a chapter in his life. Helplessness engulfed me and I sat in silence.

His voice trembled as he said, "Sookan, don't look so sad and dark. I will never stop thinking of you. Nothing will end; nothing ever does. Everything good that touches our lives becomes part of us forever. You know that." I nodded in silence.

"We'll always be friends," he said. "We're taking the same path, you know: you will eventually go to the convent, and I will be at the seminary. We will help others, and in doing so, our lives will be rich and meaningful. Who knows? Maybe someday we will even work on the same project together."

I managed a small smile and asked, "When are you going into the seminary?"

"Oh, I don't know. I have met with the Fathers there already. Now I must wait patiently. When they call me, I will go."

I heard Mother coming down the hallway, and could see the glow of the candle she was bringing to us. She watched us as we gazed at the sunset, and said, "You know, Junho, I often think of the fine hymns you and Sookan used to sing."

"Thank you," he said pensively.

Mother placed the candle on my desk and walked out. Junho and I both realized that it was now time for him to go. It would not be proper for us to chat unchaperoned in my room any longer. I knew my brothers wore disapproving scowls as they anxiously waited for him to leave.

There was so much I wanted to talk to Junho about, but we didn't have the time.

"I'd better go before I get you into trouble with your mother and brothers."

I stared helplessly at the flickering candle. I wished he could stay just a few minutes longer. As if he read my sentiments in my gaze, he sat down again. In silence, we both watched the candle burning, shedding hot tears of wax.

Sadly, he softly whispered, "I must go." He turned to the door and walked out of my room.

I desperately wanted to say, "Let's see each other just one more time before you enter the seminary." But I couldn't utter a sound. My mouth was parched, and my lips glued tight. My body trembled with sadness and anger. *Why can't we sit and talk? What is wrong with that?* I thought.

I rested my gaze on his broad shoulders and followed him with my eyes. I thought of the happy days when I stood next to him and reveled in the sound of our voices ringing through the chapel. Quickly I caught up with him in the hallway. "Did you sing much after I left the choir?"

Stopping briefly, he said, "No, I dropped out of the choir when you stopped coming. I haven't sung once since. I don't think anyone else can sing with me as you did." Then he smiled, knowing how happy he had made me.

My family and friends were still in the dining room, and we could hear low murmuring and the sound of silver chopsticks clinking against each other. When Junho reached the alcove by the front door, he slipped on his shoes and took a long look at me, as if for the last time. "You've gotten so tall. You almost come up to my shoulders now," he said as he moved to my side, just as we had always stood in choir. "Well, good luck on your test," he added with a forced smile.

He opened the door and ran down the stone steps. Without uttering a word, I followed him. When he reached the bottom, he kept walking without looking back. I stopped and watched as he disappeared into the darkness.

Rubbing my teary eyes, I wanted to shout, "Come to visit me just once more, or maybe we can meet somewhere!" But suddenly I felt it was all hopeless. What was the sense? What good was one more nervous visit? I would be leaving for a faraway place and he would be going his way.

Slowly, I walked back up to the house and closed the wooden door behind me. I stayed in my room watching

the city lights, knowing that Junho was out there somewhere, walking back to his dreary boarding house. The
candle had almost burned out, and the smell of the
burned cotton wick pervaded the room. I touched the
puddle of wax at the bottom of the candle dish. It was
warm and soft. This was the candle that had burned for
Junho and me, giving us light by which to see each
other. I collected the pool of wax, formed it into a small
round ball, and sat playing with it for a while. I was
relieved not to hear foot steps coming toward my room.
Even the next day, no one said anything about my special visitor. Although my brothers were curious and concerned about the visit, they seemed to know that Junho
was too dear to me to even be discussed.

Chapter Twelve

With our diplomas in hand, we listened as the under-classmen sang a farewell song to us. Many of us wept as we launched into our school song for the last time. Our high school years had been difficult ones. They had been interrupted by the war, and we had lost many friends. Standing side by side on the bleachers, we all noted how small our class had become, and how many teachers were missing. But no one dared mention them. We just looked at each other with resignation and understanding. There was a lump in my throat as I thought of leaving Ewha, but my mind quickly began to race with all the things I still had to accomplish in order to go abroad.

I had filed all the necessary papers with the Ministry of Education and I had gathered all the recommendations, transcripts, and health forms for the application to college in the United States. My scholarship had already been arranged by Father Lee. But I had learned that before I could even take the government test, I was required to have either a diploma from a four-year liberal arts college or a two-year certificate in science and economics. Although I had already been accepted at Ewha University, I quickly enrolled at a smaller college where I could obtain my science and economics certificate in a year by taking extra night classes. For the next twelve months, I immersed myself in my studies.

I was finally able to join the hundreds of applicants at the test site. I entered a room full of men. Some of the older men glared at me, seeming insulted that a girl dared to be there. A proctor rushed toward me and yanked my papers from my hand to make sure that I was in the right place. I was finally allowed to take the two-day test. On the first day, I had to answer questions on history, economics, science, art, music, and current affairs. The second day was even more grueling than the first. I had to write several long essays in English explaining my proposed course of study and my life goals, describing how my studying abroad would benefit both my host country and my native country. I wrote diligently until the bell rang. I was the last one to leave the testing room.

For two weeks, I anxiously waited. Finally, the names of those who passed were posted on the big bulletin board at the Ministry of Education. I had passed! Amidst the long list of men's names was my own. My brothers were so stunned that they called the Ministry of Education to make sure that it was not a mistake. Everyone had thought it would take several tries. I knew that they had hoped I would give up, join my friends at Ewha University, and then join the convent to be with my sister.

Once my passport and visa were issued, I needed to leave within the week, and everyone busily helped me prepare for my trip. Mother invited all my relatives, neighbors, and Ewha friends for a big farewell party. Teacher Yun brought me a scroll painting of the mountains. "Hang it up in your room," she said. "I don't want you to forget our beautiful Korea." Bokhi brought me a thin gold ring. She slipped it onto my finger and said, "A friendship ring. You will make so many new friends, but you won't forget me, will you?" Mother prepared four silk Korean outfits, called *Hanbok,* for me. One for each season. She carefully packed several embroidered hand towels and tablecloths that she had made. "Whenever you go visiting, do not go empty-handed," she reminded me. She tried to muster a smile, but her eyes were tear-filled and her lips quivered. "It is hard to send my daughter so far away, but you will come back."

The days were busy, filled with goodbyes and hundreds of errands. But Junho was always on my mind. I dared not mention him, not even to Mother, yet I often thought of taking a walk to Dongkuk University in the hope of running into him. I always stopped myself, though, as I knew it would not be proper for me to go there. My mother and brothers would be appalled if they ever found out. I would ruin my reputation by going to look for him; young ladies did not do that. I just wanted to be able to say goodbye to him in person, but I didn't know how to bring up the subject with Mother.

As we were packing my things one evening, Mother

saw me staring over at Dongkuk University through my window. "You want me to help you look for Junho at Dongkuk, don't you?" she asked.

Tears filled my eyes, and I nodded with relief and exhaustion. All the months of intensive preparation for the exam, and now all the last minute preparations to leave my home were overwhelming. I felt so tired and lost that I sat and sobbed.

"You cannot be weak now," Mother said, lifting my chin. "Your life is just beginning. You will have to be brave. Studying abroad will be even tougher than passing the government test." Then she hugged me and whispered gently, "Are you sure you want to leave home?" Wiping my eyes dry, I nodded.

"Well, let's see then. Tomorrow morning, after your brothers leave, we will go to Dongkuk University and ask for Junho. It would not be right just to leave without saying goodbye to him." It sounded as if Mother were trying to convince herself.

The next morning, everyone had left early except for Inchun, who seemed to be dawdling. When he finally headed to school, Mother and I hurried off on our private mission. I was surprised she had offered to help me. I knew it was not right for her to be going to the university to look for someone else's son. It just was not proper. I was lucky Mother understood. It would be our secret.

Instead of taking our normal route, we went down a back road. It was faster this way, and we were less likely to run into people we knew. It was hilly, but it was a delightful walk and the air was fresh with the smell of pine trees. We arrived at the back entrance of the university administration building.

I held Mother's hand as we walked to the front of the building. I was happy that she understood me so well, but I couldn't help feeling guilty for putting her through this. Mother hesitated as we walked into the building and saw a sign on the door that read, "Dean's Office." She stood up straight, took a deep breath, and said, "Well, I guess I am going in."

As she carefully pushed the door open, the young secretary sitting at the desk looked up through her thick glasses. "Can I help you? Are you lost?" she asked as she rose to her feet.

Embarrassed, Mother said politely, "Oh, no, we are not lost. I am very sorry to disturb you, but I wonder if you could help me. I would like to see the dean."

"He is very busy now. If you tell me the nature of your visit, perhaps I can help you," she said quizzically.

"I believe Junho Min is a student here. If possible, we would like to see him for a minute or two," said Mother.

"Oh, Junho Min. Are you his mother?"

Mother shook her head.

"His aunt?"

Mother shook her head again with her lips tightly closed. "We are not related. We met Junho during the war, when we lived in Pusan. We would like to see him, but if that's not possible, we understand. I am sorry to have disturbed you. We should go." Mother turned.

"Wait, maybe I can ask the dean. Wait!"

A minute later, a tall, bespectacled, silver-haired man stepped out into the reception area. Taking off his glasses, he bowed to Mother and said, "I hear you are looking for Junho Min. He is one of my favorite students! But he is no longer here. He left about two weeks ago for the seminary. He joined the Franciscan order. You can find him there, on the other side of the city." He bowed again, and returned to his office.

Mother seemed grateful that he had not asked who we were or why we needed to see Junho. "What a kind man! I'm not surprised that he was so fond of Junho," she said.

We walked down the paved road and out the big gates of the university. The streets, filled with shops and restaurants, were bustling with students. I saw groups of students sitting in the small restaurants eating hungrily. I looked at the rows of boarding houses that lined the side streets and wondered which one Junho had lived in.

We headed toward the station on Ulgiro Street and squeezed onto a streetcar. The streetcar rattled down the narrow roads, stopping periodically to let people off. We passed the East Gate of Seoul City and proceeded all the way to the far end of town. We were the last ones on the trolley, and got off at the very last station. In the distance across an open field, I saw a large, gray, stone building cloaked in haze. It took us a good half hour to walk through the field of tall grass and wildflowers.

Finally, we reached a paved road lined with poplar

trees. The somber stone building stood before us. It was unharmed by the ravages of war, and looked immune to the happenings of the world. In its austere perfection, it seemed sacred and forbidden.

We walked through the gate and slowly approached the heavy wooden doors of the large building. Mother looked at me. Do we dare to enter? she seemed to ask. I didn't know, and waited for her next move.

She pushed the door open, and it let out a loud squeak. My palms started to sweat, and my heart raced. We shouldn't have come, I thought to myself. I saw no one, yet I felt as if a million eyes were on me. Suddenly a black crow squawked overhead. I jumped and, yanking Mother's hand, said, "Let's go home. I made a mistake."

Mother held my hand tightly and pushed the door open a bit more. We peeked in and saw an inner courtyard. Tall lemon grass grew around the perimeter, and the yard was dotted with low stone stools. It was so quiet in there, I could hear my own heart thump. A pair of big dragonflies flew overhead and the sweet scent of the grass filled our lungs. "Come, let us tiptoe in and see," Mother said, and we bravely stepped inside.

Bees buzzed in the far left corner where roses and tulips were in bloom. In the middle of the garden, a small fountain gurgled softly. In front of us was a row of round, flat steppingstones leading to a gatehouse with a small, latticed window. Propelled forward by the neatly arranged steppingstones, we proceeded. Behind the latticed window was an old priest reading his prayer book with his head bent low.

We stood quietly, waiting for him to finish his prayer and notice us. After a while he closed his book, looked up at us, and came outside. His long black robe swished against the overgrown grass surrounding the stepping-stones. He lifted his eyebrows expectantly.

With hesitation, Mother began, "Father, please forgive us for disturbing you. We were told Junho Min is here. We know him from Pusan. If it is possible, we would like to see him for just a few minutes to say goodbye."

The old priest looked calmly at Mother and said, "I will report to my superior. Please wait." He turned and disappeared through a door.

Would the priest bring Junho back with him? Or would he tell us to go home? And if Junho did come out to see us, what would I say? Would he be embarrassed? Would I be getting him into trouble? I wondered what he would look like in that long black robe. I hoped I wouldn't cry when I had to say goodbye.

Mother nervously looked down at her clasped hands. I was not a good daughter to make her go through all of this for me. But how else would I be able to say goodbye to Junho? If I had gone looking for Junho alone, I would have brought shame on him and myself and my family. With Mother along, it seemed as if we had some serious business to attend to. Besides, I had promised Mother that I would never keep a secret from her again. This was my only choice.

Confused, guilty, and embarrassed, I looked at Mother. Seeing how worried I was, she smiled and said, "I am fine. I wanted to be here with you, remember?" I reached out for her hand. Together, we walked toward the little fountain and sat on the low stone stools nearby.

I watched the streams of sunlit water shoot up, and then burst into thousands of little droplets that played on the dazzling rays of the afternoon sun. Each drop sparkled a different color, creating a magical liquid rainbow. As the delicate droplets fell, others rose to sustain this luminous rainbow. There was a soothing, rhythmic splash as the descending droplets met the water's surface. Watching this rainbow, I felt peaceful. I swung my legs against the tall lemon grass. It tickled. The rainbow seemed to whisper, "Junho will be glad that you came. Your mother is not upset with you. Everything is as it should be."

I thought of how Junho must sit here every afternoon, watching the water. I didn't need to worry about what I would say to Junho. There would be no need for explanations or excuses. There would be no regrets and no tears. It would be enough just to see him again and to smile. He and I would know we had an everlasting friendship. In this garden, I was sure that all would be understood without words.

I saw a shadow, and I promptly stood and turned. It was a different priest, tall and slender. As Mother and I bowed, he nodded. His arms were folded in front of him, and each hand was tucked into the opposite sleeve. He wore a gentle smile as he gazed upon us. After clearing his throat with a quiet cough, he said, "I understand you have come to see Junho."

"Yes, Father. If it is possible, we would be most grateful," Mother pleaded on my behalf.

Unfolding his arms and clasping his hands, he said, "Junho and I both appreciate your taking the trouble to come here. We know why you are here. However, it is best not to disturb Junho just now. He is doing well. Be assured that he is doing what God has asked of him. Go in peace, Sookan and Mrs. Bak. You will be in our prayers."

He stepped forward, placed his left hand on my lowered head, and blessed me, making the sign of a cross with his right hand. Then he did the same for Mother. He smiled at us, crossed his arms again, tucking his hands into his big sleeves, and disappeared.

Overwhelmed, I plopped back down on the stone stool. The sun hung low in the sky, and the shadows of the tall poplar trees fell across the garden. We were not that far from the city, and yet, I felt as if we were a million miles away, a million miles from all the worries and sorrows of the inhabitants of Seoul. It was a piece of Heaven here, and I was happy that Junho was a part of it. I appreciated the priest's kindness. I could still feel the way his pale, delicate hand rested gently upon my head. His blessing made me feel safe and special. He must be close to Junho. Maybe he was Junho's teacher, his confessor. He apparently knew of our friendship, and spoke for Junho. I was sure he would tell Junho of our visit when the time was right. Perhaps it was better this way, to never say goodbye. Perhaps it was Junho's way of telling me that everlasting friends have no need to say goodbye.

Chapter Thirteen

The following week, I boarded a plane for the States. Peering through the small airplane window, I could see everyone waving their handkerchiefs. Mother, in her crisp, white *Hanbok*, waved when she wasn't wiping tears from the corners of her eyes. Standing next to her was Teacher Yun, who vigorously waved her large white handkerchief. "Sookan is the smallest one in that line," I had heard her whisper to Mother as I boarded the plane. "She is too young to go so far away from home." "You know her," Mother had replied with a tremble. "So determined to study in America. No one wants her to go." Father Lee stood on the other side of Mother with his arms crossed as he stared at the plane.

Hanchun, Jaechun, and Hyunchun, dressed in their dark Sunday suits, looked somber and still rather stupefied. That very morning, I had heard Hyunchun say, "I still can't believe that little one is really leaving us all for a place where she knows no one." I watched them, standing side by side with their hands in their pockets, staring at the plane in silence.

Bokhi and my other friends from Ewha were clustered around the bus that Hyunchun had rented to bring them to the airport. They chatted amongst themselves while waving at me all the while. There were so many little things I wanted to say to each of them.

Then I looked over at Inchun, who stood all alone. He was always so stoic and reserved, yet I knew how sensitive he was, and how it must hurt him to see me go. I wished I could run down, give him a hug and bring him onto the plane to come away with me. I remembered that he had slipped something into my pocket as I was frantically saying my last goodbyes to my Ewha friends. I hurriedly reached into my pocket and found a small slender package. It was a thin, silver fountain pen. In a note, he had written, "*Nuna*, a writer should be a good correspondent. Write home often. Inchun." He did not say that he would miss me or that he loved me, but I knew how often he would think of me and how deeply he would always love me. I was glad that I had thought to hide a note for him under Luxy's drinking bowl. I had oiled and sanded Luxy's bowl so often that it now looked like a rather unusual modern sculpture. The grain of the cherry wood complemented the curve of the bowl, and I liked feeling the smooth roundness. I had asked him to take care of it for me.

As the engine started to rumble, tears filled my eyes. The plane taxied away and I watched all of them wave their handkerchiefs until they looked like dancing snowflakes. I was suddenly filled with fear and remorse. Would

I ever see them again? I was going so far away, to a place none of them had ever been before. I cried in silence for a while, with my nose pressed against the small pane of glass. I was lonely and afraid. Would anyone love me in the States? Would I have any friends there? I was going all alone to a vast country where I would be surrounded by total strangers. What had I done? Why had I never thought of it this way before?

Below, I saw the tip of a brown mountain peeking through the cloud cover. I thought I saw the shouting poet standing there with his hands cupped around his mouth. "Good morning, little girl. Good morning!" his strong energetic voice rang out.

Fluffy, steel-gray clouds passed before me. I looked out at the sky, and I thought of the rainbow I had seen in the garden of the seminary. I imagined sitting by the gurgling fountain with that rainbow dancing before me. I imagined Junho's tranquil and gentle smile. The bright sun appeared through the traveling clouds and sparkled against my window. I leaned back and closed my eyes.